the

SASQUATCH
MURDER

(a love story)

the

SASQUATCH
MURDER

(a love story)

JEFFERY VILES

— Beaver's Pond Press —
Minneapolis, MN

Edited by Wendy Weckwerth

ISBN: 978-1-59298-769-6
Library of Congress Catalog Number: 2017908018
Printed in Canada
First Printing: 2017
21 20 19 18 17   5 4 3 2 1

Beaver's Pond Press, Inc.
7108 Ohms Lane
Edina, MN 55439–2129

(952) 829-8818
www.BeaversPondPress.com

To order, visit www.ItascaBooks.com or call
1-800-901-3480 ext. 118. Reseller discounts available.

SasquatchMurder.com

The lonely business of imagining a story and putting it on paper, or nowadays first on a screen, is impossible to accomplish without encouragement and suggestions from friends and professionals within your circle. To those I enlisted for such help, and you know who you are, your many kind words and intelligent observations are deeply appreciated. And to you, dear reader, as the well-used address goes, I hope above all that you enjoy this fiction. It strives to occasionally use interesting language to tell a simple but lively tale that's enjoyable to read. There is a continuing mystery. Are they real or not?

When Darwin published his conclusion that man was descended from an apelike ancestor who was again descended from a still lower type, most people were shocked by the thought. . . . One of the hardest lessons we have to learn in this life, and one that many persons never learn, is to see the divine, the celestial, the pure, in the common, the near at hand—to see that heaven lies about us here in this world. . . . One thing is inevitably linked with another, the higher forms with the lower forms, the butterfly with the grub, and the flower with the root. . . .

—John Burroughs, "The Divine Soil," 1908

PROLOGUE

At the beginning of beginnings there was only ∞, which was darkness multiplied by nothingness. The darkness was eternal and unchallenged until ∞ divided nothingness by zero. A sound not unlike a faint brass trumpet note pierced the void, and light issued forth. Darkness could not subdue the light. Whatever was not darkness was light. The future had a future. Within the light were particles that contained excitable atoms held together in an electron cloud. Some of the particles providentially embraced, improving themselves to become matter. The matter improved to become all the things we see and know. From the light and then the matter, each thing created itself through an irresistible force, an urge. All this taken together is what we call God. All of it is God. Everything that exists can be seen as part of what we call God. The God who was God before the light and the particles, and then after. God did not ask for the job because the only thing to ask was himself. In this way, all things came to be. As unknowable billions of years passed, every part of existence—whether an atom, a quark, an amoebic proto-fish, or a galaxy—had experiences, learned, and changed to better itself. Stars created themselves in uncountable numbers. Some exploded and sent their particles scattering through what had become a universe. Those particles became all that exists, including us. Each of us is part of a star and part of God. One distant day, it all will cease to be. The light will collapse into the darkness. All that has ever been will be no more.

As the creation urge continued, some sixty million years ago, beings we now call primates began to walk on what we now call Earth. They had experiences. They changed to their own betterment. And down through the unfathomable tunnel of time that separates then from now, the primates taught themselves to come down from the trees, stand upright, and outwit the competition. A simian self-consciousness ignited and began to evolve. Hominids ruled. *Homo erectus* prospered for two million years and then died out, unable to improve itself sufficiently. *Homo sapiens* survived by eating meat protein to grow a larger brain and take control of the magic of fire. Seventy-five thousand years ago in what is now called Indonesia, a supervolcano erupted in a magnitude unknown to historic times. Everything changed. Light dimmed. Plants struggled. Species died. *Homo sapiens* came close to extinction. Modern humanity might never have existed, but about two thousand of the biggest-brained *sapiens* survived. These individual Africans were the direct ancestors to modern man. Sixty thousand years ago, they actuated a storm of behavorial change. They developed the ability to visualize things that weren't in front of them and make pictures of those things on cave walls. They began to communicate with each other by a system of primitive sounds. They began to bury their dead and be curious about the night sky.

The great ice retreated. Animals migrated into the newly fertile hills and valleys. Our ancestors followed them. Some *Homo sapiens* were relatively advanced when they sashayed out of Africa into Europe and across southern Asia. Some weren't so advanced, but followed along. They walked together, female and male, advanced or not, across the Bering Land Bridge fifteen or twenty thousand years ago, learning that in groups they could hunt down the dim-witted mammoth to provide rich, fat-laced meat and the beginning of good humor around a fire. These early hunters spilled into North America, which was a game park of bison, horses, camels, giant ground sloths, saber-toothed cats, bears, and many other creatures that didn't know what to make of the invaders. The humans eventually established native groups from Alaska to the Amazon, wherever there were animals to kill and roast and eat. Consciousness advanced. Many of these early humans experienced a geometric increase in mental activity, including a rudimentary inner life. Some became reflective. They were wetting their feet in the river of idea and thought that, far downstream, would produce Mozart's music, computer code, nuclear warfare, and *Gilligan's Island*. Not all things were consistent, however. Imperfections occurred. Now and then a gene was not turned on, a chromosome was bent, a synapse did not fire. Thus, a large but defective member of a small group stole meat from the others. He established a maverick cult that didn't follow the rules that had been developed through eons.

Some fourteen thousand years ago, on a windswept ocean's rim near what would come to be known as Vancouver, stood two groups of hominids. One was a group of twelve. The other numbered nearly three hundred. A large male stood at the front of the bigger group and faced the other dozen. He made a series of head shakes and throaty, one-syllable sounds followed by the sucking of air through clenched teeth. He pointed a thick finger toward the deep and ancient forest beyond. The smaller group was cast out, its witless members cursed to fend for themselves. They would live or die on their own. Remarkably, the castouts did, indeed, survive. But they evolved and improved very little compared to their brethren, though they did become physically large and astonishingly secretive. And they continued reproducing into our own time. Certain of the Pacific Northwest native tribes, themselves begat from the larger group on that prehistoric shore, came to call them Sasquatch.

1

THE KING OF STORMS

El Niño was to blame.

The sheltering clouds began to waltz at three in the afternoon, transforming a batting of cotton puffs into a scud of charcoal. A freshening wind lifted leaves and sent them skittering across the loamy forest floor. New thunderheads leapfrogged until they straddled the horizon and formed an angry scrum, churning with energy. The retreating sun was beaten and soon gone for the day. A polite spittle of rain quickly became a deluge. The firmament opened with the first crackle of lightning. It seemed like the king of storms, a biblical rain caused by the warming of a current far out in the Pacific. The afternoon sky became dark and ominous, the color of a bad bruise. The gentle spring temperature fell. Lightning strobed the woods like an antique kinescope and illuminated wind-rippled sheetwater spreading over the landscape of enormous trees—firs, hemlocks, Sitka spruce, Pacific yews, and western red cedars.

Some of the giants survived in old-growth forests and soared hundreds of feet into the air, resigned to their destinies and locked in their assigned positions since well before Balboa came snooping. They broke the falling water with their wide arms and siphoned it through the canopy to the layers below. Sluices of gurgling water knifed through leafy gutters and created waterfalls to the ground, which carved ruts in the soil that revealed gnarly complexes of roots and the occasional arrowhead.

The hail began with vigor and rat-a-tatted a drumroll through the woods. Then it stopped suddenly and left a swath of packing peanuts melting into the ground. Earthworms writhed to the surface for air. Jake Holly and his horse had hurried to the carveout of a two-hundred-fifty-foot Douglas fir tree when the downpour began. The tree stood on a fir-mantled hillock, its gap cauterized by lightning a week before Lincoln was shot. Man and horse, mutual enablers for thousands of years, squeezed together in an effort to escape nature's petulance. Horse breath is never honeysuckle, but Split Log's had a gamy edge that caused Jake to take umbrage. "Splitty, your breath would peel wallpaper," he said as if his horse understood English. "You've been in the wild onions again."

They settled inside the tree. Jake brushed away bug shells and sat on a clump of damp wood shavings. He propped his aging Henry .44 upright and turned his face away from the horse. They loved to roam the old woods together. Jake carried the rifle when they did, but he wasn't a hunter. It rarely had been fired. The weapon's purpose was comfort. It was protection and connection—protection against the unknown and connection to the old days. It was passed down from his grandfather, a deer hunter, who'd hand-whittled the stock from swirly, bird's-eye maple. The Henry threw a slug that could stop a grizzly, if necessary.

Though it seemed impossible, the rain intensified.

Jake looked out from his woody cave toward Mount St. Helens, some twenty miles to the north and slightly west. He saw nothing. The heavy rain obliterated any view of the brooding mountain and its plume of steam and ash. In the past few days the volcano had come to life after decades of silence following the apocalyptic eruption of 1980, when it furiously blasted away its lovely dome and north flank. Back then, the mountain rumbled awake again after sleeping for more than a century. It shot its stream of fire and ash and pumice and gas fifteen miles into the heavens, killed fifty-seven people and countless wildlife, and leveled hundreds of square miles of dense forest land. As with prehistoric volcanoes, the eruption turned day into night. The ash cloud formed a girdle around planet Earth. Car owners from Denver to Jakarta wiped away a milky glaze, wondering what had clouded their paint. Schoolchildren got a current-events lesson in geology. A few were actually interested.

Now the mountain was now burping its way back to life as miniature earthquakes shook its flanks. Volcanologists agreed that nothing predicted another dangerous eruption like 1980, but area residents kept a watchful eye on the rattling lava scree and periodic steam clouds being ejected.

The day had been a good one for Jake and Split Log until the rainstorm. Sheltered in the dampness and faint light of the tree gap, Jake closed his eyes and allowed his synapses to rewind. He thought of his early-morning jog and remembered how he'd startled an antlered buck along the trail. Many of Jake's days began with a two- or three-mile jog from the organic vegetable farm that was his home into the small town of Aurora, Washington, and back. As a blue-chip ex-jock who had lettered in both baseball and football at his Missouri college, at age forty-two Jake battled to stay in shape. Except for the usual wrinkles and a little soreness from time to time, he was holding his own. He looked young and felt younger. His athletic features were intact and his dark, shortish hair was staying where it belonged. Jake's striking girlfriend, Jessica O'Reilly, daughter of the county prosecuting attorney, thought he was six feet of hunk and kindness. Jake was a complex man, a closet polymath with catholic curiosities. His mind probed unexpected alleyways from Japanese gardens to fine wines, from orchid arrangements to the violin lessons he had recently undertaken. Jake was fascinated by things most people rarely consider—a human being's endless emotions, the special joy in a life of the mind, and the quirks and mysteries of the nervous system.

His move to Washington from Missouri and his farm had saved Jake's life after he became a youthful widower. Allie was his match. Fun-loving and outgoing, she was step for step with him as they established four Live Right Express restaurants by age thirty-five. But life hands out lumps, as Allie used to say, and "we can only hope they stay in our mashed potatoes." Allie's did not. Her lump was on the X-ray, and it explained why no children had arrived. The rest was breathtakingly fast. None of the treatments worked. Usually Jake forged ahead with an indomitable confidence, much like the thunderclaps rolling through the northwestern forest that day. But when he lost Allie, that confidence—his soul, really—left the building. The arc of Jake's grief was wide. His eyes had a thousand-yard stare. His mind was pocked and dented like a car in a hailstorm. Only lately, six years after her death and half a continent away, was he beginning to feel healed—thanks to the farm and to Jessica. Jake possessed a heart shattered by Allie's death and slowly stitched back together with root vegetables and barbed wire. Earlier, the day's spring warmth and sunlight and green growth underfoot had felt to him like a resurrection of hope after a cold winter.

The rain continued to rend the cumulus and dive to the earth. Inside the tree cleft, Jake half dozed. In his reverie, he sensed the emotional presence of Jessica with her whipped-cream skin and heartbreaker freckles under boyishly cropped, red-blond hair. Split Log, originally named Bird but rechristened after he kicked and splintered a rotting stump, stood motionless and serene, as horses do.

2

TRUTH OR LEGEND?

For centuries, the big footprints were found both by native Indians of the Northwest and, later, by whites who came to harvest timber. When Europeans arrived, they learned the stories of *Saskehavas* from the Salish Native Americans. Eventually, the word morphed into English as *Sasquatch*. Wherever the whites settled and mingled with the natives, from the Kwakiutl of British Columbia and the Athabascans of the Yukon River to the Hupa of the Northern California redwood forests, they encountered the same tradition of Bigfoot sightings. A giant, hairy, humanlike creature dwelled in the great woods.

The first mountain men ran their traps in the early nineteenth century and emerged from the old growth with tales of the ape man. Later, Teddy Roosevelt explored the area and wrote of a trapper he'd heard about who was kidnapped by one of the beasts. Pioneer miners and fishermen told similar tales of Bigfoot confrontations and, in one instance, of shooting a Sasquatch and then being attacked by his mates. Down through the decades of the twentieth century, the huge tracks continued to be found, along with the occasional tuft of inexplicable hair and convincing anecdotes about close encounters. Many skeptics became believers.

Eventually, a cottage industry was built around the Northwestern Bigfoot. Assemblies of enthusiasts overran campgrounds and bought kitschy souvenirs, like whittled monsters or plaster casts of supposed footprints. The result was a substantial boost to local economies. Hoaxes abounded, including famous film footage purporting to show the creature and a deathbed confession from its creator admitting fakery. Scientific studies were conducted, but they didn't clarify the picture. Some studies argued that while Bigfoot might be possible, such as surviving remnants of the huge primate *Gigantopithecus* from the Pliocene era—which is well known from fossil remains in Asia—how could such a creature exist even in small pockets and avoid discovery through the centuries? And where were the skeletons and scat? Other studies of equal luster posited that an intelligent creature that desired to escape detection could do so most of the time, and that more and more believable sightings from credible witnesses were testament to mankind's increasing presence in the Sasquatch environment across the toe of the Cascades and the Pacific coast to the north. Furthermore, such studies opined, we don't find skeletal remains of dead bears or mountain lions either because they're eaten and scattered by scavengers, such as coyotes and ravens, plus they decompose rapidly in the damp north woods along with the scat. Deer mice are especially effective at recycling the raw calcium of bones, believers suggested, while reminding skeptics that natives' tales of mountain gorillas in Rwanda were disbelieved until the creatures were outed by western biologists in 1902. They weren't studied for another half century.

Aurora wasn't a place populated exclusively by true believers. It was divided like the rest of the region. Some believed. Some didn't. Some placed the stories in the netherworld between myth and reality. But having the Bigfoot legend certainly didn't hurt business now that monster tourists showed up. Even the local nonbelievers weren't above making a buck off the lore during the annual Bigoot Festival or joining a heated debate over a frosty mug.

After all, monsters have been part of human experience from the dawn of recorded history. A misshapen, huge Grendel waded the marshes in *Beowulf*, which is among the oldest examples of English literature. Aurora stood squarely in that tradition. Much of the time, it mattered little whether a creature existed or not. If he didn't exist, the locals would surely miss him. The maybe–maybe not phenomenon was real enough, never mind an actual beast tromping the woods. If Sasquatch didn't exist, a little self-deception was convenient and profitable.

3

THE .44 HENRY SHOT, "AN ACCIDENT"

The creatures were disoriented by the storm as they heaved themselves through the enclosing brush. They had a heightened awareness about weather, partly due to a sense of smell that trumped the most alert of canines. They would shelter themselves well ahead of a normal rainstorm. This rain was not normal.

The female creature had eggplant-shaped breasts that swayed as she walked slightly behind the enormous male. He was the better part of eight feet tall and four hundred pounds. The pair moved into some bushes and overgrowth not a hundred feet below Jake and Split Log. They were well proportioned and seemed at home among the oversized trees and green, textured carpet on the forest floor. They shook and bent some branches into a rough enclosure. Had someone been witness to their nesting, he would have noted their caution and tenderness. They treated each other with deference, two calm giants pulling away offending limbs and piling them together to form a place to lie down. The creatures were hairy, to be sure, but less so above the shoulders. Their expressions and ministrations to each other did not seem apelike.

But there wasn't a witness. Jake was dozing and Split Log was in a full horse trance. The rain washed out any sound or smell that might have revealed a presence.

As the two Sasquatch lay down, they created a muted snap of wet twigs that opened three eyes, one belonging to Jake and two to Split Log. The horse's nostrils widened and twitched, but he smelled nothing suspicious. Jake pursed his lips and raised his head slightly. He heard only the driving rain raking the ground and bubbling through the gullies. Each of them sensed the other felt no alarm. They relaxed.

The male Sasquatch nuzzled the female as they tried to shelter each other. Their bright eyes communicated. A trace of a smile crossed the female's countenance. Aside from the size and hair, the creatures could have been teenagers on a lovers' lane.

———◆———

Jake thought the heavy breathing was his horse. His brain waves quickened while emerging from a light sleep in the tree hideout. He realized the rain was letting up. In a moment, he began to depart from the calm limbo between asleep and awake. His first movements to stand made the horse instantly alert. Now they both could hear the deep, low breaths and rumblings from the brush below the rise where they were sheltered.

Jake knew it was a noise he hadn't heard before, and whatever was making the sound was not something he knew about. Years of roaming the forest surrounding Aurora made Jake as knowledgeable as any local woodsman. A surge of fight-or-flight adrenaline caused him to raise the rifle and unlock the safety as he leaned forward to peek out from the tree. When he moved, Splitty emitted a low grumble. It was enough. The male Sasquatch heard the noise and rolled off his mate. He stood and looked toward the huge Douglas fir with the large cleft, carefully pushing aside the mantle of green growth they'd collected as their shelter. He saw the man and horse and instantly raised his chin to loose a piercing howl. It had a volume and pitch and length that made Jake's heart skip a beat and then race.

Jake didn't aim his rifle, but he felt his reflexes push it toward the howl. He was unaware of pulling the trigger, but there was no other explanation for the Henry's loud crack, which made Split Log bristle, rear, and scramble out of their tree cave. There was no other explanation for the hole that appeared in the big Sasquatch's shoulder or the other hole that appeared just above the female's left eye. There was no other explanation for the second roar the male issued, a deafening growl, or for his attempt to rouse the female who lay crumpled at his feet, or for his unsuccessful effort to pick her up with only one useful arm, or for his thrashing farther away through the brush and abandoning his companion while bellowing with hurt and rage.

The trigger was pulled. Jake pulled it. It was blind instinct, and he regretted it before the big slug exited the barrel. But there was no changing what happened. Split Log

17

backed away from the scene with a continuous babble of whinnies and slobbers.

Jake stood just outside the tree, bending over and taking long, slow breaths with his eye on the retreating Bigfoot. His ears rang with tinnitus from the gunshot.

There was nothing else to do at the moment. On cue, the last sprinkles of the deluge hissed through the leafy canopy. The sky began to reveal the expiring day. The troublesome steam cloud issuing from Mount St. Helens was visible again.

4

UNLIKELY CORTEGE

Jake leaned against the tree and stared down toward the Sasquatch body below. He could make out parts of her face and both breasts through the thick brush. "Oh, no," he whispered over and over. "No, no, no." He looked in the direction the male had withdrawn and saw moving brush and a dark body that confirmed, as did the diminishing huffs and howls, that the creature was moving farther away. Eventually, he heard a low, throat-clearing gurgle from Splitty, some thirty yards back. He called on the gelding to return. Slowly, after much cooing and coaxing, the nervous horse responded and came close enough for Jake to take the reins. Both of them eyed the brush and its contents below. Split Log pranced his hooves and tossed his head with assorted complaints, as if he knew what was coming next even though Jake didn't.

As he absorbed that the startling events were reality, Jake began to navigate the possibilities and form a plan. He was never accused of being a true believer when the subject of Bigfoot came up, as it often did, but neither had he sided with the disbelievers. In a heated discussion at Hee-Haw's

Tavern less than a week earlier, Jake had said, "Boys, leave me out of this one. I'm a Bigfoot agnostic and an abortion agnostic and a capital-punishment agnostic. I've seen tracks in the woods I can't explain and neither can you. But if they're out there, why hasn't someone found a carcass or a skeleton? Maybe one of these days we'll know for sure." That day had come. Knowing that scavengers would find the corpse after dark, Jake saw no realistic choice other than trying, somehow, to get the creature's body back to town. Assuming she was dead.

A good fifteen minutes passed before either man or horse felt inclined to move down the hillock for a closer look. The creature wasn't moving or breathing, but caution was the prudent course. Jake decided that about an hour had passed since he took shelter from the storm. He supposed he must have dozed in the tree for fifteen or twenty minutes and wondered how long the creatures had been lying just below him. If his guess was correct, it was about four thirty on a Friday afternoon in May, though he could tell little about the time by looking up. The sky was now as biblical as the rain had been. Angelic light slanted through scrambled-egg clouds as if heaven were using an X-ray machine.

Sooner or later, Jake realized, he had to take a close look at the Sasquatch. He felt sure she was doornail dead. He tied Split Log to a large stob and drew from a reservoir of physical courage carved into his ego from athletic battlefields. Instinctive caution gave way to doing what needed to be done. He picked his way a hundred feet downhill, rifle in hand. He pulled back a wad of brush. His heart pounded. He leaned closer to take a look. It was a moment he would remember all his days.

The first unexpected thing he noticed was her grooming. She had partially clean fingernails and head hair that looked roughly combed. She didn't look like a wild animal, dirt-caked and disheveled from a hard life outdoors, but brought to mind a homely, hardworking mother of six from a mud-puddled trailer park somewhere in the backcountry. However, she was larger, much larger, and covered in thick and unruly body hair. But the humanness of the creature startled him. He drew back and took a deep breath to calm himself. He knew immediately the lore of Sasquatch' rank odor was a myth. There was only a faint smell, slightly wild and a tinch gamy. He sniffed again and detected only the blood smell a hunter might expect from a fresh kill.

Jake took a closer look. Her coif reminded him of flappers from the 1920s, crudely shorn into a bob. Though Jake was astonished to see it, the creature's hair appeared to have been cut with something, straight across the back at shoulder length and pulled away from the face. The eyebrows were thick and wiry but only slightly raised, not nearly as much as an ape's would be. The neck and face were less hairy than the rest of her. Below the shoulders and elsewhere, especially below the waist, the hair was dense and reddish brown. Her face was slack jawed, with an open mouth that displayed her teeth. Jake expected to see rows of huge, razor-sharp pickets but instead made out uniform rows of molars and incisors. The canines, however, were very large and very sharp. They weren't proportional to human teeth. They reminded Jake that this had been a large and dangerous creature. The weight of death, the reality of death, was evident in the open mouth and heavy permanence of her repose. The bullet hole above her left eye was small, but under her head Jake could see blood and tissue from the exit wound splattered on the wet ground and leaf bed. Her body was splayed, head tilted to her right shoulder, with huge breasts, a thick waist, and, yes, big feet.

Jake noticed her privates and was embarrassed that her labia were spread. He realized the pair was copulating just before the shot was fired. Another flush of regret swept over him. He had killed her dead, forever and ever. He had taken away everything this creature ever had. He backed up a step, ran his free hand through his hair, and shook his head side to side. "Damn, damn, damn it," he said. Jake stepped backward and to the side, bent over, and vomited onto the mossy forest carpet.

Two things were clear. He didn't want to leave her to be torn asunder and eaten by big-woods carnivores, but getting her back to Aurora wouldn't be easy. In another minute, a plan had formed in Jake's practical mind. He set about fashioning a strong travois, the simple litter used by Plains Indians to carry supplies and people behind a horse. He pulled Split Log to the body, talking to him reassuringly. He urged the horse to sniff. Splitty at first wanted to keep his distance but eventually became accustomed to the dead creature. It helped that her odor wasn't strong. Judging from her appearance, the creatures tried to clean themselves with some regularity. And the El Niño rain had provided a thorough shower. Split Log smelled the ground, the air, the brush, and finally the corpse itself before being convinced there was no danger.

The horse grazed on young shoots while Jake worked at making a stout and springy travois from thick, moist branches. About half a mile away, an abandoned logging trail twisted through the trees for another mile until it joined a back road headed in the right direction. He guessed they were six or eight miles from Aurora. They had wandered cross-country through the forest maze, so he couldn't be sure. Jake had told Jess he'd be back around dark to take her to Hee-Haw's for supper. That wasn't going to happen.

It was Jake's habit to carry a few supplies in Split Log's saddlebags. The serrated hunting knife, rope, hatchet, compass, packages of dried food, tent roll, matches, and canteen of water gave him a sense of security. The rifle was along for the same reason. He could stay overnight in the woods if it were ever necessary. Under the circumstances, the supplies became essential and were the focus of Jake's attention.

He first cut the trail poles for his travois, measuring them to cross over in front of the saddle horn. The simple frame structure, shaped like an isosceles triangle, had been used by prehistoric people and, eons later, Native Americans to haul heavy loads with animals doing the pulling. A wheel needed a road, but a travois could go anywhere. Jake knew this one had to be strong. He cut pieces of his tent rope while he talked softly to Split Log, explaining to the horse and to himself what had just happened. He lashed the poles together in front of the saddle and sharpened the trailing ends. He cut four cross braces to strengthen the frame and added two vertical ribs to make the platform into a lattice, tying the whole affair together with the rope pieces and double square knots. It was definitely strong, but Jake couldn't be sure it would work.

Split Log looked up from his grazing from time to time and swung his head around to watch. The horse had never pulled anything and was suspicious of the travois. But he was smart and well trained, and he understood there was no choice in the matter. When the sled was ready, Jake positioned it next to the Sasquatch body. He had managed to roll the creature onto some of his tent canvas, which he used to slide her away from the enclosing brush.

While moving the body, he saw that the exit wound on the back of head was the size of a silver dollar. Most of the bleeding had ceased. He tucked up her legs, tied her into a bundle, and covered her by the tent material. Then he began the difficult process of pushing and pulling and rolling the bundle onto the travois. Jolts of adrenaline were helpful. Jake thought about what he was doing and cursed softly to himself. Periodically, he looked across the woods in the direction the male had disappeared but saw only trees and brush in the fading light.

The tent had metal-reinforced holes along its edges, and Jake found he could gain purchase and leverage by running a piece of rope through a couple of the holes, then looping it around his saddle horn and using it as a pulley. The rope scraped along Split Log's haunch and the horse protested, but eventually, inch by inch, the corpse was on the travois. Jake tied it tightly to the frame. The travois sagged, but held. Jake examined the ground where the creature had died. He took out a plastic Ziploc and scooped up bits of Sasquatch tissue, bone, and blood from the ground. He put the bag, knife, and other supplies into the saddlebags and rerolled the remaining tent canvas. He fed Splitty a double handful of dried apricots and rubbed the horse's neck and withers. "Are you ready, big boy?" he asked. "Let's roll."

The pair and their cargo began to move. Jake walked ahead, leading Splitty through the path of least resistance. The travois worked beautifully, knifing efficiently through the wet forest floor.

The weak light from the rain-beaten sun was fading fast as nightfall fell. Jake guessed the time to be six thirty and knew that darkness loomed. The moon had little chance of reaching the forest floor through the pointy lushness of the big pines crowd. The limbs and needles released delayed droplets of moisture to fall to the loamy earth like an artillery fusillade, and the big-woods smell was rich and ripe and as piney as a grandma's sprayed bathroom. Jake wasn't worried about getting lost because his hand compass would point the way and his penlight had a fresh battery. But already the ancient forest was taking on a foggy and gloomy cast that made him nervous. The big male Sasquatch was formidable. The creature occupied an unfamiliar space in Jake's psyche. The fear of the unknown passed down through untold generations of *Homo sapiens* reminded him of his frailty. He was wary and watchful, safer because of his caution. Wind-swayed limbs rubbed one another and made groaning noises. They sounded like a wounded Bigfoot. Jake's gooseflesh kept him alert.

He reminded himself that the male was wounded, and he had a powerful rifle. He reached again and again into his reservoir of discipline, the mother of courage, and kept moving. Large insects worried the damp air as Jake and Splitty dragged their unlikely package. As Jake swiped at a deerfly that looked as big as a teacup, he reminded himself he was doing the right thing.

He'd shot a Bigfoot. That couldn't be changed. It was an accident, completely unintentional. He couldn't leave her to scavengers, and her body was important to science. He would take her back. Split Log was hyperalert but calm, as long as Jake talked to him. The air was cool and quiet from the rain and darkness. The procession advanced to the logging ruts ahead.

A century and a half earlier, tough, hungry men felled big trees and dragged them with mules to local sawmills that popped up like mushrooms. It was a hard way to make a living. Most of the early loggers departed broke and disillusioned before the federal government bought up much of the land to preserve it. Some of those men died in the woods. Local tales of logger ghosts were common around Aurora, and tonight Jake wished he'd never heard them. Twice he thought he saw a dark form nearby that could have been a Sasquatch. His heart raced as he strained his eyes into the gloom and held the big rifle aloft. Once, he fired into the sky to declare his potency. The horse danced and voiced his disapproval. Jake paid constant attention to the load on the travois, keeping it balanced in the center, and Split Log made steady progress along the mossy ruts. When they left the logging trail and mounted the dirt road, the pulling got harder. The road was packed with mud after the rain. The sharpened trailing poles dug into the dips. The horse was sweat-caked, and his bite on the bit was foaming despite frequent stops to drink from the puddles. They kept moving. Jake was glad for the scraping noise the travois made. It warned anything out there, logger ghost or Bigfoot, of their approach. Visibility was poor and getting poorer as the wet fog continued to creep between the tall trees.

Jake stopped his improvised cortege along the outback road and thought maybe he'd gone far enough. The last thing he wanted to do was injure Split Log. Aurora, he guessed, was still two or three miles away. Spending the night along the road wouldn't be pleasant, but it might be his only choice. He thought constantly about Jessica during the ordeal, hoping she wouldn't be too worried. That was unlikely. She knew the general direction they were exploring that day, and he'd wondered if—maybe even hoped—she might come looking. Then he saw faint headlights piercing the somber darkness. What were the chances her gut would tell her something was wrong and she needed to drive the pickup into the night down a muddy road? What were the chances Jess would be behind the approaching lights? One hundred percent, as it turned out. Exactly 100 percent.

"Hey, you strange and crazy man," she said as she pulled alongside. "I've been worried sick after that rain. Why are you walking? Is the horse OK?" There was rose water and crème brûlée in her voice.

Jake reached into the truck and touched her cheek. "You will never, ever know. . . . I can't even begin to tell you . . . how glad we are to see you. Tonight you're our guardian angel. Get out carefully. We've got something to show you."

Jess stepped down from the 4×4 and deftly executed a jump and hug and then planted a firm kiss on Jake's sweaty lips. "I'm sure glad you're all right," she said. "I was starting to think up all kinds of things." She walked toward the heavy-breathing horse. "Jake Holly, what on earth have you been up to? What's this deal strapped on Splitty?" She stopped when she saw an indistinct parcel roped to the litter and backed up a step. She could see something furry under the canvas. "Talk to me, Jake. Are you really OK? What's this? A bear?"

Jake clicked the penlight on. "Now come over here behind me and stay calm, please. Don't be afraid. It's dead. First, I want you to know it was an accident. I didn't intend to shoot it. Here, take a look."

Jess looked over Jake's shoulder as he parted the tent material and illuminated the face. "Oh good God," she said as she flinched her head backward. "Is that what I think it is? Jacob, Jacob. I don't believe it. What are you going to do?"

"I'm not sure," Jake said quietly, shaking his head. He hugged her again. "Forgive me, love. I doubt if I smell much better than Splitty's breath. We've been working hard. This happened so quickly I didn't know what to do. I knew I couldn't leave her out there. Let's try to load her in the truck and then figure out what to do next, OK?"

They unshackled Split Log and removed his saddle and bags. They put the travois and horse gear in the pickup, gave Splitty a drink from the canteen, and treated him to a handful of dried apples. The hydraulic tailgate made it easier, but not easy, to load the creature and its shroud into the truck bed. They tied the horse's reins loosely to a side mirror and crept toward Aurora. Relieved of his load, Split Log kept up nicely. For a while, neither Jake nor Jess said a word. Once they started talking, they couldn't stop.

"I can't believe this is happening," Jess said, her heart still hammering. "Are we crawling through the dark with a dead female Bigfoot in the back?"

"We are. I wish we weren't, but we are," Jake said.

"You seem sad. I know it was an accident. I believe you. But why are you sad?"

"You couldn't see her very well, Jess. She looks almost human. Her fingernails are clean . . . well, not clean, but not like claws either. Her hair is cut across the back. She looks more like a cave woman than a wild animal. The horse and I were inside a big tree hiding from the rain. It rained like crazy. I couldn't see anything, not even the mountain. Did it rain much in town?"

"Two or three inches in no time. It was like a waterfall. Good old El Niño, they keep saying. I was worried about you caught outside, but I convinced myself you would find shelter. Sounds like the rain was only part of the problem. Whenever you're ready, tell me what happened."

Jake was driving. The headlights trying to pierce the road were overwhelmed by fog. He said nothing for a moment, just stared ahead and drove slowly. He stopped the vehicle and flipped on the cab lights, looking directly at Jessica. "When we saw them, the adrenaline hit me like I was struck by lightning. Everything happened so fast there wasn't time to think. My stomach felt like it wasn't there," he said. "Like there was a hole in the middle of me."

"When you saw . . . them?" Jess asked. "More than one?"

"There were two, male and female. During the storm they were going at it right below us in the brush, the way it looked. I was more or less asleep, and I guess Splitty couldn't smell them for the rain. They ended up thirty or forty yards from us under some creambush and saskatoon, on a nest of maidenhair fern. When the rain let up, we heard something, like heavy breathing. When Splitty whinnied, there was this

God-awful howl. I was coming out of my nap, and I just shoved the gun toward the howl by instinct—and somehow, I don't know how, must have pulled the trigger. In another second or two, I'd have been awake and had my wits. I'm sure I would have shot over their heads or, more likely, they would have moved away on their own. When I saw what happened, I threw up."

"You didn't do anything wrong, Jacob."

"I know, I know, but I wouldn't have pulled the trigger if I were awake. It was like a bad dream, and it happened so quickly. I really didn't know what was going on—and then it seemed like it was over before it started. If the rain hadn't been so thick, or if I could have clicked awake an instant sooner—if I'd even had a moment to think—but by the time I was awake, the shot was gone.

"It makes me feel terrible. I carry my Granddad's rifle for insurance. You know I wouldn't harm a rabbit or cause any creature to quit this life if I could help it." Jake put the pickup in gear but didn't move.

"Jake, listen to me. I know you wouldn't shoot anything, and I can tell you're stressed, but you're being too hard on yourself. Accidents happen."

Jake looked at Jessica's lovely face in the glow of the faint dome light and smiled at her. "I'm feeling a little fragile," he said. "I'm tired, Jess, and ready for a shower and some food." He laid his head on her shoulder.

She kissed his hair and scooched around him under the steering wheel. "I'm driving," she said as she released the brake and eased down the road. "Tell me where we're going."

5

OSCAR'S FUNERAL HOME

For seventy-six years, the Oscar Marsh Funeral Home had served its patrons well. Jonas Marsh migrated to Aurora late in the logging days. He used the training his father had provided back in Ohio to establish the only funeral home in the region. His son Oscar, a third-generation mortician, added his first name to the business and followed his father's maxims every day since Jonas passed: wear a black suit and tie, be earnest with the bereaved, and get the fees up front. With a few people like Jake, however, Oscar allowed his lighter side to bubble up. Nobody ever had a better friend than Swampy, the nickname Oscar's friends had derived from the last name *Marsh*. He shared an interest in wines with Jake. They often split a bottle, sometimes more, over gin rummy and male needling at Jake's house. Jessica dialed Oscar on her cell phone and handed it to Jake as the couple, the horse, and the extraordinary corpse arrived in Jake's driveway outside Aurora.

"Swampy? Jake. Glad I caught you."

"Hey, pal. Tonight's not a wine night, is it? I was watching crocodiles eat wildebeest on the Discovery Channel."

"No, it's not," Jake said. "I've got something I need help with. It's pretty urgent. I've got a little . . . well, you might call it a problem, or at least a situation. Could you meet me at the funeral home in ten minutes? And don't say anything to Helen."

"What am I supposed to tell her? She's already making the popcorn." Oscar's wife was named after the famous nearby mountain and sometimes shared its testy temperament.

"I don't know, but you'll understand when you get there. Tell her you forgot something. Tell her you'll be right back. You won't be gone long. I'm asking you to trust me on this one. Your cold room isn't full, is it?"

"It's empty, actually. And of course I'll trust you, but this is starting to sound serious. Is everything OK?"

"Swamp, we're fine. Jess is with me. Just meet me there in ten. I need a little help."

"Fine. I'm on the way."

The pickup crunched to a slow stop at the barn, and Jess and Jake got out to untie Split Log. They led the horse to water and hay and tossed a blanket over his back.

"I'll be back to brush you, Splitty," Jake said, patting the big roan gelding on the neck and looking him in the eye. "Right now, we're in a hurry."

Split Log issued a murmur of gratitude at being home and began to drink deeply from his trough.

They drove to Oscar's with Jake behind the steering wheel. Jess looked at him calmly and waited for an explanation of his plan. Her pale green eyes sparkled and her reddish-blond hair shone. As always, she was alert and yet gentle as a baby bird.

"You heard me talk to Swamp about his cold room," Jake said, "so you know what I'm thinking. We don't need decomposition. I'd like to hear your opinion."

"Well, yes, on what you're thinking," she said. "Obviously, you're taking this dead Sasquatch we're hauling around—and I can't believe I'm saying this—to put her in the funeral home. I'm with you so far. What I don't know is, what happens after that? What happens tomorrow, or the day after tomorrow?"

"I wish I knew. I've been thinking about it since I realized the travois would work, but I still don't have answers. Let's take it one step at a time. I wish she weren't back there, but she is. I couldn't leave her for the coyotes and bears and buzzards. Step one was getting her back to town. We've done that. Step two has to be keeping her intact and the whole deal quiet until we figure out step three. I can barely imagine how the zoologists and paleontologists and every other kind of ologist will run with this. We need to park the body with someone we trust. Oscar's cold room will keep her for now. Do you have another idea?"

"Nada," said Jessica. "I guess we could go bury her somewhere and not say a word. But you're right, the scientific value has to be enormous. She's also probably worth a lot of money somehow. We can trust Oscar, right? But if he tells Helen, it's all over town."

"We can trust him. I don't see that we have any choice. I know you're right about her being valuable. That occurred to me, but I'm absolutely sure that's not the reason I went all nuts to get her in. It's hard not to jump ahead. Let's get her to the cold room and try to figure out the next step. You OK with that?"

"Of course I am. I hope Oscar's gurney will hold her."

6

BILLY THE SPY

Oscar was unlocking the funeral home's back door and fumbling for the outside light when Jake and Jess drove up.

"Hey, Swamp. You might want to douse that light," Jake said as they exited the truck. "The less attention we draw, the better."

Oscar clucked his tongue. "Lordy. What are you getting me into, Jake Holly? Hi, Jess. If you two don't take the cake. You look as serious as cancer." He switched off the light. "OK, let's hear it."

Jess snapped on the penlight. "Come back here, Oscar," she said.

Jake took Oscar by the arm and guided him toward the truck bed. "Swamp, I'll tell you the whole story in a sec. Jess is right. First, you'd better have a look for yourself."

They pulled back the tent canvas and shone the small light on the Sasquatch's face. Oscar leaned in to see, then jumped back and sucked in his breath. "Great God Almighty," he wheezed. "What in the name of heaven is that? I hope to hell that thing's as dead as Hermann Göring. Damn, Jake, is that a Bigfoot? Is that a bullet hole in its head? Did you shoot it?"

"Sorry for the shock, Swamp. Yes, she's dead. And, yes, she's a Bigfoot. And, yes, I shot her. Here, pull this back and take a good look," Jake said. "It was an accident. Splitty and I were holed up in a big fir tree during the storm. I was snoozing a little, and before I knew what was happening, her mate was howling at me something terrible—and I shoved the rifle in their direction, and it went off. It's a miracle I hit anything. I knew I had to bring her in. That's why we need your help. We need to put her in your cold room until we decide what comes next." Oscar looked the creature up and down by the penlight Jess held.

"Well, my Lord," Oscar finally said. "I've heard every one of the stories a hundred times. I've seen the footprint casts and read about the hairs they couldn't figure out. I've lived here all my life and thought I was open-minded about it, but until this moment I didn't really believe they existed. I've even been to many a circus and rodeo, so it's not my first trip into town." He looked up and grinned. "This takes the cake. You said there was a mate. What about him? And how in Sam Hill did you get her out of the woods?"

"I'll tell you the rest inside, Swamp. Right now, let's see if your gurney will hold her."

"It'll hold her. It's made to hold a three-hundred-fifty-pound man and a heavy casket. We need to put some rubber gloves on first. And it's gonna take all three of us."

The trio disappeared inside and returned wearing gloves and pushing a gurney. They left the outdoor light off but switched on a small sconce just inside the door.

———◆———

If El Niño was to blame for the storm that smothered all sound and odor and caused the Sasquatch pair to lie down in front of Jake's tree, it was also to blame for Billy Lasswell being twenty feet up a sugar maple across the back street from Oscar's. The torrent had flooded Edgar Lasswell's basement two blocks away. When Edgar came home from his job at the lumberyard, he'd already stopped with his buddies and sucked down a six-pack. When he saw the basement, Edgar launched into an alcohol-fueled tirade.

At twelve, Billy knew when to come and when to go. He couldn't trust his father to direct his anger at the rain and the broken-down house. He feared being recruited to bail water half the night. Billy slid out the door and up the street. He was afraid Edgar would come looking, so he climbed the tree and was quiet. He saw the goings-on across the street from his perch. He saw the penlight and people looking into the pickup bed. He saw them go inside and return and then struggle to load something onto the gurney, cover it up, and wheel it inside. He could see through the glass door into the hallway when an enormous, hairy arm slipped from under the canvas and was quickly tucked back in.

Billy noticed an inside light in a corner room go on. He was already out of the tree and moving toward the building when he saw the mini blinds in that room being closed. By standing on tiptoes at the window, he could peek through the corner of the window since the blind didn't fit tightly. Oscar's father had bought it thirty years before at a discount store in Olympia and hung it himself. So Billy had a partial view to a small room inside where they wheeled the gurney and pulled back the canvas. What he thought he saw made him swallow hard.

He watched as the three people quickly examined the creature before one of them turned on a refrigeration unit and covered the gurney with a rubberized sheet. When they shut off the light and prepared to leave, Billy ran. He ran fast, but he didn't run far. As Billy crossed the street and passed his hiding tree, he felt himself rise in the air. Something had snagged him. He thought it was his father, still on the rampage. He was wrong. His racing heart stopped cold when the male Sasquatch pulled him up and examined him through intelligent eyes. The boy was scruffy and dirty from tree climbing, he needed a haircut, and his Walmart clothes were twisted and disheveled.

When his heart started pumping again, Billy saw the mud poultice on the creature's shoulder. The Bigfoot moved his face to within inches of Billy's in the misty, foggy dark and made a low sound in the back of his throat. He raised Billy up with the uninjured arm as if to cast him to the ground and kill him. The Sasquatch paused and tilted his head back. He released an even lower sound that seemed to come from his stomach. Thunder grumbled in the sky, and a light rain began anew. The creature looked at the ground and saw trickles of water already washing away his huge footprints.

He set Billy on the ground and pushed his head with a huge finger as if telling him to go. The boy was paralyzed for a full five seconds but soon burst away and hit top speed by the fourth stride. He didn't run toward home and his father's problems. He ran toward his best friend's house a half mile away. As he ran, his jumbled thoughts raced a million miles an hour.

7

HEE-HAW'S—BEER AND STORIES FLOW

"OK, I'll meet you back here at seven in the morning," Oscar said as the three prepared to leave the funeral home. "I hope you figure out how you want to proceed because when this gets out, the spit's gonna hit the fan. I think you already know that."

Jake shook his friend's hand ceremoniously. "That's exactly what we intend to do, Swamp. We'll be here bright and early, especially for a Saturday. Look, I know Helen will want to know where you've been. What will you say?"

Swamp released Jake's hand and looked at his shoes. There was a moment of awkward silence. "Jake, you know she's a good woman and we have a good marriage."

Jake nodded.

"I'd rather tell her the truth," Swamp said. "Imagine how it would be later on if I didn't. She'd know I hadn't trusted her."

"You're right," Jake said. "You're completely right. But can you get her to keep a lid on it for a while? Maybe explain to her we're trying to figure out how to handle things and if the news gets out we've opened Pandora's box?"

"Yes, I can. She'll zip it if I ask."

"Fair enough. See you in the morning."

Motors combusted to life. Vehicles departed. Jake told Jessica he was in urgent need of a shower, a couple of beers, and some food—in that order.

Jess said she'd like to wash up too, especially after handling a Bigfoot, and that Hee-Haw's Tavern sounded good to her. They drove to Jake's comfortable ranch house and cracked open two Olympias thirty seconds after walking in. Jake showered, and Jess washed her hands, face, and hair quickly, but with gusto. Both brushed their wet hair casually. Jake wasn't the sort to let his hair cause trouble, and Jess took no nonsense from hers, either. She tied it into an I-don't-care topknot worthy of a double-crested cormorant while Jake hurried to the barn to groom and feed Split Log.

Within thirty minutes, they opened the heavy oak door to Hee-Haw's and saw a steady blaze alight in the fireplace. Despite the mild temperature, the air was heavy with humidity and fog. The fire felt good against the dampness. The tavern's nondescript, wide-boarded exterior, which fronted Main Street, displayed only a neon donkey for identification but gave way to a wide and welcoming interior warren of booths, mismatched tables and chairs, a pool table, and the requisite glowing Wurlitzer. The air wasn't smoky. Hee-Haw had installed a venting unit on the ceiling and, in any case, the town council would soon vote to ban smoking in public places. The bar was nearly full at eight thirty this Friday evening.

"Hey, there," Hee-Haw bellowed from behind the bar. His voice could scatter a murder of crows, and his eyes gleamed with mischief, like he was about to shake your hand with a joy buzzer. "Here comes a pair to draw to." Albert Swearingen hadn't said anything quietly since second grade, and he'd been known as Hee-Haw for many years. The nickname came from his favorite joke, which concluded with a stutterer repeating, "He-aw, he-aw, he-aw, he always calls me that," and sounding like a donkey's bray.

"What'll you have tonight, my little chickadees?" Hee-Haw asked.

Jess and Jake grinned. "Two from the tap, dear boy," Jessica teased in an English accent, "and a matched pair of your greasiest cheeseburgers, if you please—hold the foie gras."

They glanced around the tavern and nodded at friends while awaiting their beers. As usual at Hee-Haw's, the crowd represented a diverse cross-section of local humanity. The place was one of those rare American gathering spots that compared well to a good pub in Ireland—the sort of joint that might contain a butcher or a senator, and where the chances were equally good of hearing a filthy joke or a soliloquy on existentialism. There were always a few nonlocals in attendance, usually Bigfoot acolytes making a pilgrimage to the Holy Land. Aurora, and a few nearby towns in southwest Washington, were considered Sasquatch central. There was a surprisingly good motel in town—the Bigfoot Inn, of course—which capitalized on a Paul Bunyan motif. The owner would invariably recommend Hee-Haw's to his guests for decent food and well-told tales. "You may be a stranger when you walk in," he would say without exaggeration, "but you won't be when you leave."

Jake and Jess carried their mugs to a far corner booth. It was next to a bookcase groaning with paperbacks and painted a shocking shade of cobalt blue, compliments of leftover auto paint donated by a car dealer. They spoke to nearly everyone they passed. Jessica waved cheerily toward two men sitting at the end of the bar. They were lawyers and so was she, having started her own firm doing a brisk business defending the accused, even though her father was the prosecuting attorney. As Jess herself was fond of saying, if a town is too small to support one lawyer, it can always support two. They greeted house painters, a carpenter, business owners, two pals of Edgar Lasswell's from the lumberyard with their wives, a lady stockbroker, and several young men and women from a nearby junior college preening and inviting later upchuck by downing Jell-O shots. Jake and Jess settled into the booth. They spoke to each other in soft voices designed to blend into the general hum.

"The longer I think about this, the more it takes my breath away," Jess opened the conversation and stared intently into Jake's eyes. "I'm sure you realize there must be people all over the world who'll want to know. They'll want to study her, take her away. This is huge, huge news."

Jake nodded as Jess spoke.

"One phone call and every network and newspaper will knock each other down to get here. Have you decided how you want to proceed?"

"Yes. I'm leaving tonight for Mozambique," Jake deadpanned. "I'll be back in six months. Seriously? I'd rather not handle it. But I guess it wouldn't help to disappear. God, you look luscious tonight. I love the topknot."

Jess grinned without inhibition and said, "Thank you, sweet."

"There's no simple way to explain that body lying over at Oscar's. Most of me wants to go bury her somewhere, but that's a cowardly option. I feel like you do. It's exciting to know they exist, but I truly wish it hadn't happened. Can you believe how human she looked? That shocked me as much as anything. I don't want to have to explain how it happened in front of a camera, with TV suits and talking heads asking the same questions over and over."

"And that haircut," Jess said.

"No kidding. They'd have to really sharpen rocks to do that, unless they found some old scissors out there and learned how to use them. Is that even possible?"

"A lot of the stories say there's a bad smell," Jess said. "I could never figure out if these creatures were so elusive, why would they give off a bad smell? Mother Nature doesn't work that way. Their prey would smell them. Or smell where they'd been, what they'd brushed against. All they ever find are footprints. I thought she just had a woodsy smell, didn't you?"

"Exactly. When I first approached her in the brush, I couldn't smell a thing. Of course, the rain made a difference. You had to get really close to smell her at all. Even then, it was more like a horse or a deer. Maybe if they know how to cut hair, they know how to take a bath."

"Yup," Jess agreed.

"Now that we know they're real," Jake said, "imagine how secretive they must be to keep from being found or photographed. Other people besides me are running around out there. Keeping the odor down is something you'd do if you didn't want to be discovered. Did you notice her fingernails? They weren't that bad. They almost looked like she'd tried to clean them." Jake sat quietly for a moment, pondering, and then tried to summon a more cheerful mood. "Come to think of it," he said, "if you shaved off some of that hair, she'd look a lot like your aunt Louise."

"My sainted aunt," Jess emoted with her best high-Shakespearian inflection. "I know you're kidding, but you may be right." She cocked her head and teased back. "You are kidding, aren't you? Of course you are. But we mustn't go there. Even if you're right, you're wrong. Mustn't talk that way about darling Daddy's darling sister."

"Why not? He hates me anyway. He makes it almost a Hatfields-and-McCoys atmosphere."

"He doesn't hate you. He doesn't even dislike you. He just thinks you're too old for me." Jess took a deep breath and sighed dramatically. "And you are somewhat elderly. Tell me, beloved, do you have an AARP card? Can't you get us a handicapped parking sticker?"

"OK, girlfriend. I deserve that for the crack about Aunt Louise." Jake took her hand and squeezed it like he was testing a pear. "I'm glad it was your cradle I robbed, my little Irish rose. Now, let's get to it. What are we going to do?"

Jess shrugged and pointed her palms upward in the universal I-don't-know signal.

Jake continued. "Speaking of your dear dad, several people around would prefer not to hear about a dead Sasquatch through the rumor mill, and Talburt O'Reilly is at the top of the list. I know he's a fine lawyer and prosecutor. He's probably even a good dad, considering how you turned

46

out—except for your needling of the elderly. But he's not partial to being out of the loop."

"What would you suggest, then? Run over to the house and tell him about it?" Jess's eyes narrowed. "We both know he's been reserved, to say the least, about us becoming a couple. Auntie Louise married an older man who turned out to be a drunk and a wife-beater. Why he connects that to you, I don't know. But he does. I think he'll get over it, but until then, I'm giving him some room."

"I wasn't thinking of rushing to his house or inviting him to join us for high tea," Jake said. "I was thinking you could loop him into this and let him know it was my idea to include him. That couldn't hurt, could it? You could ask him to meet us at Oscar's in the morning—and then, I don't know, maybe he could honcho a local press conference or something. We could shoot a video of the corpse, take measurements, blood and hair samples, that kind of thing. Then comes the hard part when the rest of the world finds out: the town blows its lid, and I'm in a horror movie."

Jessica paused and sipped her Oly before replying. She smiled at Jake, and it warmed him. "As usual, you're making sense. Bringing Dad on board would be a good thing, especially in his eyes. And the video is a good idea. But I'm having trouble digesting a local press conference. What would it be, just the local paper? What about the TV stations from Olympia, Seattle, and Portland? If there's going to be some kind of official announcement, why not go all the way? Ask CNN, *USA TODAY*, the *New York Times*, the *Washington Post*? Make it a big deal now because sooner or later . . ."

"Exactly," Jake said. "It makes no sense to spread it through the good, old *Aurora Advertiser*. Maybe your dad would have ideas. Maybe I can get enough brownie points with him to thaw things out. Good Lord, I dread all this. It sends a shiver through me to think what will probably happen. What if people don't believe it was an accident? What if they think I tracked her down and shot her through the head?"

"No one will think that, Jake," she said. "People around here know you better than that." Her face lit up in another huge smile. "Guess what? This, too, will pass."

———◆———

Billy Lasswell sprinted the half mile to Chuck Wooten's house with his feet barely touching the ground. His body weight vanished when the creature sat him down. He felt like he was flying, not running. He was glad Chuck was on the porch watching the rain when he sailed into the front yard and began babbling so fast he might have been speaking Urdu. Chuck calmed Billy down and kept him away from his parents until he got the full story. Then he told his father. As his dad picked up the phone, Billy and Chuck started searching the Internet.

———◆———

Back at Hee-Haw's, the evening was rife with the customary atmosphere of beer-fueled gaiety. Bad jokes competed with strong opinions among the local citizenry, who mixed laughter and dispute in equal doses. At a red vinyl booth, three college boys in the bloom of youth sniggered when one of them announced he was "trolling for nooky."

One of Hee-Haw's barmaids stopped by the table. She was fair skinned and her eyes were as dark as lumps of coal on a snowwoman. Her impossibly lean midriff was exposed to display a gold navel adornment.

It was time for the troller to troll, or suffer the slings and arrows of his pals. He launched into an explanation to the barmaid of how he'd heard about growing marijuana plants right out in the open, simply by hanging red Christmas tree bulbs on them. "From the police helicopter," he said, "they look like tomato plants. When they search the fields, they just fly right on by." He posed with his most winning smile.

"Yeah, right," the barmaid said with a smirk. "I'm so sure that would work." She rolled her dark eyes in doubt and moved away.

At the lumberyard table, a sturdy man in a green corduroy shirt troweled butter to bread and explained how he gave his brother $10,000 for his birthday every year. His friends waited for the other shoe to drop. "And then on my birthday two days later he gives me ten thousand, and we deposit the checks on the same day." He stretched his arms with a satisfied look, as if he'd just invented the wheel.

In a corner sat a large woman with a kidney-shaped wen, an unpleasant growth, on her neck. The small man who sat across from her was her husband. Though her amplitude highlighted his modest presence, the man radiated an air of calm authority because he was well dressed and well groomed, and his expression was peaceful. She was talking, for the thousandth time, about the shameful things her drunken father had done to her after her mother died.

At a tall, oak bar table on the margin of the room sat a scarred man with perfect ears. His original pair had been badly disfigured in a fire. He ran a pet cemetery and was affectionately known as Doug the Dead Dog Dude. His sister and her husband sat with him. Two years before, the sister had begged her husband for a sum of money he couldn't afford but loaned anyway. The cash was for sending Doug to a Hollywood prosthesis expert she'd read about in *People* magazine. The movie man fitted him with sculpted silicone ears hand painted to match his skin tone, then refused any payment.

Near the bar sat three men in casual clothes and a woman dressed as if she were having her picture taken. The men tried to outdo each other in political right-wingedness. A short, heavy man had the floor. He had popcorn stuck in his teeth and rolled his tongue like a lizard just finished with a grasshopper. His beery breath staled the air. His face was scrunched tight, like a wadded piece of paper. "Here's what you do with them suicide terrorists," he proclaimed. "You give them terror right back. You dip what's left of them in pig's blood and bury them facedown. Them sheet heads don't like pork, and I hear they got to be buried a certain way or they won't get their virgins in heaven. That might discourage them quite a little bit. In fact, why don't we drop pigs on them instead of bombs? I reckon they might have trouble cleaning up the mess. That'd be terror, wouldn't it? Imagine getting whopped upside the head with a pig dropped out of a B-52."

"You got that right," said a tall, crew-cut man with a dangling cigarette. The smoke wafted upward and made him squint until his eyes looked like watermelon seeds stuck in his head. "I'll go you one better. We oughta cut off a pig's head and scoop out the inside and slide it over the head of any terrorist we find, dead or alive. Let them feel the slime and try to see out the eyeholes. Get Al Ja-what's-its-name TV to send out pictures of that kind of a deal. Bet the liberals would love that." He leaned back and sucked on his Winston.

"I hate to bring it up, boys, but wouldn't something like that put us right down on their level?" The speaker was the female at the table, a regular known as Spoon because she was always stirring things up. She was a psychology professor at the junior college. The good ol' boys at Hee-Haw's simultaneously admired her and fought her tooth and nail, always in good humor. Part of their admiration stemmed from her thirst. She matched them beer for beer.

"Here we go," said a man in a flowery camp shirt who ate well-done steak every evening. He was called T-Bone. "Spoon's gonna go Commie on us. What should we do with terrorists, then, madam? Put them in jail and feed them? Maybe get you college professors to rehabilitate them? On second thought, that might not be a bad idea. Let's put terrorists in the lockup out at Supermax in Colorado, where we put the worst of the worst, and let them deal with the gangsters in there." T-Bone grinned at Spoon.

"All that steak is backing up on you. It's clogging your brain," she needled, grinning back. "If we put terrorists in jail, more terrorists will line up to hijack a school bus and demand their brothers be released. I don't claim to have all the answers. It just seems like if we give away our freedoms and terrorize other people because we're mad, they win and we lose."

"As usual, Spoon's got a point," said a new arrival, a man with thick glasses and a half-chewed cigar. "The trouble with talking about terrorists is that everything's upside down. You can figure out a way to deal with folks who value life like we do, even if they're enemies. But how do you deal with wackos who intentionally kill as many people as possible to try and force us back to the fifteenth century? These people have some goal that's revealed only to them by their God, and the rest of us are infidels who need to be murdered. No discussions, no negotiations. You need to fight terror with terror—cell by cell, wherever they are—until something changes. A lot of people don't like fighting, and that includes me. But I'd like to hear a better idea." He shrugged and tightened his mouth into a half-kidding, half-serious smile. "Let's bring out the pig heads."

Back and forth the conversation roiled as the glassware clinked. Some of the notions volunteered were thoughtful, others vexing, a few downright irritating. The subject of Bigfoot was broached, as usual, concluding with the customary split decision.

An alluring blonde in her late forties wearing a red dress so tight she looked shrink-wrapped was telling two women friends at her table she'd been on a diet since she was nine. "Vicki, you're out of your freaking tree," said one of the friends. "You've never in your life been one ounce overweight. You eat anything you want and never gain. I hate you for that."

"Well," said Vicki, "thanks—I think—but even if that's true, I need a little cushion going into old age. Everybody spreads out then."

At the bar, a man sporting a shaved head and a white mustache bored Hee-Haw with a sermon about toilet paper. He explained, in detail, how the bar's rolls weren't pulling over the top, as they should. "Now, Albert, how many things in this world are as clear-cut as that?" he asked. "People can always argue the other side of anything, but not which way toilet paper ought to unroll. You've got to find the little universal truths where you can. Judas Priest, how could anyone load it the wrong way?"

Hee-Haw thought about his cat that unrolled all the paper if it came over the top, a good reason to wind it the other way. But he said nothing.

"You ain't wrong, Cotton," chimed a man in his seventies wearing a fifty-year-old plaid sport coat. The older man's name was Lawton Roy, which, mercifully, had shrunk to LR when he was a boy. LR's teeth looked like a row of tree stumps logged a century ago. He had a slight asthmatic wheeze between sentences, a heart that had worked too hard, and an ingrown toenail that had been throbbing for two days. Four beers had taken the edge off the throb. "My girlfriend hangs it so it comes off the bottom. She does it just to irritate me. Hey, did you guys see in the paper about that Indian named Grover Turkeyfoot? I think he was a Cowlitz, or maybe a Suquamish. He caught a guy with his wife and knocked him out cold, then cut off one of his thumbs. When the police asked him why he'd done that, he said because the man was his friend—and otherwise he'd have killed him."

In the booth by the blue bookshelf, Jessica and Jake devoured their burgers, sipped their beer, and made plans for the next day. When they left they would call her father. They'd invite him to meet at Oscar's the next morning, without saying exactly why. At Oscar's, they'd suggest making a video and ask his advice about how to proceed, hoping he'd take the lead in announcing the Sasquatch to the rest of the world. As an elected official and experienced lawyer, Tal O'Reilly was good at making speeches and plans. Perhaps he'd want to be involved in deciding who could access the funeral home and how to handle the press.

Plus, as Jake had surmised, involving Jess's father might help thaw the cold war of their relationship. Tal had pushed the uncomfortable situation into a near vendetta. He was blind when it came to Jake. At forty-two, Jake was fifteen years older than Jessica. To Tal, that was too much. When his sister Louise had married at thirty-five, her husband was seventeen years her senior. The O'Reilly family considered it a bad bargain that had to be taken. It was Louise's first chance at marriage, and probably her last. Almost immediately there was rumor of physical violence and heavy drinking by her new husband. Then came unemployment, womanizing, and finally, absence. He went away and didn't return.

Louise was devastated but waited three years to get the divorce. She was a homely but good-natured and intelligent woman who saw her only chance for a family disappear. Louise's big brother Tal was always protective of her. He felt he'd failed her. When Tal heard the ex-hubby was living with a woman in a small Oregon town across the

Columbia River to the south, friends had to restrain him from taking a crowbar and calling him out.

With this history as a backdrop, Tal simply could not see Jake in a clear light. He nagged his daughter about the relationship. "How would kids feel about having a dad too old to roll on the floor with them?" he asked. "How will you feel walking into a PTA meeting with a guy on a cane? I'm not that much older than him, you know. Think it through."

Jake tried to show Tal in their infrequent conversations that he was aware of the age difference and would make sure it didn't become a problem. He was an extremely polite and considerate suitor. Even though Jess was an adult with her own residence and her own business, Jake wrote Tal a letter more or less asking his blessing to see her. Jess wanted to move in with Jake. Jake wanted that too, but asked her to wait because of Tal. Jake wanted to pop the question soon, but was sure bunking together would make things worse with Jess's family. Finding a way to get her father's support was important.

Tonight Jess was first to suggest, "Let's go home." She scrunched up a lecherous grin and raised one eyebrow as she said it, a familiar sexy signal between the two. Try as he might, Jake didn't possess the genetic quirk to raise a single eyebrow, so he launched into his response, an impersonation of Goofy with both eyebrows semaphoring up and down. "Yup. Uh-huh. Yup. Let's go hoooomme." They left Hee-Haw's waving at friends.

Arms around each other's backs, they walked down Main Street past Dryer's Shoe Store, Binion Furniture, and Wooten Drugstore to their parking place near Beth and

Verna's Diner, the B&V. It was known with affection as the Belch and Vomit.

"Interesting," Jake said. "Plenty of cars along Main Street but not a person in sight. Every Jack and Jill is inside Hee-Haw's. Back in Missouri, my dad used to say you could shoot a cannon down Main Street and not hurt anybody. Same way here, this time of night."

"Hey," Jess said, pulling her hand from her jacket pocket. "I forgot I've got my cell phone. I can call Dad right now if you're sure that's what you want me to do."

"I think so, yeah. Call him," Jake said. "Tell him to meet us at Swamp's in the morning at about seven thirty. You do the talking, please, but don't say more than you have to. If you decide I need to talk to him, hand me the phone."

Jess was on the phone a scant half minute before clicking off. "I'm amazed," she said. "He's not at home. Mom said he left for a while and would be right back, but she didn't know where he went."

"We'll have to call him early in the morning," Jake suggested. "He's usually up drinking coffee by six, isn't he?"

———◆———

At some point during the extraordinary events of the afternoon and evening, an unspoken agreement was reached. Jake and Jess knew they needed to be together that night. The stunning reality of an expired Sasquatch lying in Oscar's cold room made them feel fragile and in need of each other. Their habit was to be rigorously discreet about cohabitation, short of living a lie, and that meant sleeping alone most of the time. They looked forward to the rare nights when they could justify staying together. Lengthy discussions were commonplace. They analyzed what they were doing and why. Both felt strongly their toe-in-the-water living arrangement wasn't due to a lack of commitment to the relationship, but rather an acceptance of the reality of small-town gossip and the presence of a prominent and disapproving father. As long as each kept a home, they weren't living together.

"I've got some chocolate frozen custard," Jake said as he pushed the button of his garage-door remote.

"Not on top of beer and a grease burger," Jess said. "Seeing your Sasquatch made me nervous to start with. Add some chocolate, and I might not sleep at all."

As they exited the vehicle and entered the house, Jake put his arm around her waist and pulled her close. He jokingly tried again to raise one eyebrow. She smiled in collusion and poked the offending brow of hair above Jake's eye.

Jake said, "Come here, beauty. You'll sleep when I get through with you."

She smirked, and it widened to a grin. "I love it when you talk dirty." Gently and deliberately, she kissed him softly, full on the lips. "I'm going to brush my teeth, and I'm planning to brush fast."

8

HOME SWEET HOME

Daylight leaked in. The unwelcome reveille of the sun pierced the bedroom with its daily dose of reality. The first thing Jake saw in the new day's light was Jessica's beautiful hand across his chest. It was utterly perfect, small and delicate and feminine with sculpted nails and not a spot or blemish. Only a hint of blondish hair traced the sand-colored skin. "Opposable thumb" popped uninvited into Jake's sleepy brain and jostled its relaxed delta waves. Immediately the image of the female Sasquatch lying dead in the woods was back. The slow delta waves quickly vanished and were replaced with fast, alert alpha waves. The transformation took a split second. Jake gently kissed the luscious hand draped across him and tried to slide from underneath it without waking her. He failed.

"Ummmmm," Jess murmured. "That was nice. Kiss me some more. What time is it?"

"Almost six. Let's call your dad in a little while and have him meet us just after seven. Swamp will be there. I slept reasonably well, considering. How about you?"

She opened her eyes and gave him a dreamy look. "Pretty good. Surprisingly good, actually, thanks to you keeping your promise. I did have an unpleasant dream, though. Something was chasing me. I think it was a bear."

"Sorry about that," Jake said. "I had one that was odd, but kind of pleasant. Seemed like it lasted all night. There was a roomful of sleeping children, really beautiful kids. I was awake and watching over them. Every few minutes, one of the kids would give a little moan, or thrash around in bed, and I would know the child was having a bad dream. So I would tiptoe over and touch the top of the child's head and gently breathe into her hair. The child would immediately calm and go back into deep sleep. It was a wonderful power. Now that I think of it, I was dreaming about dreaming." He rolled over and held Jess close.

"Let Dr. O'Reilly analyze this," Jess said into his shoulder. "Could it be that our subject is ready to have children himself? You will let me know if I'm right, won't you?"

"You're always right," he said thoughtfully. "It's past time for me to be a father." He held her at arm's length as they both sat up in bed. He smiled a smile that made her feel good about the coming day. "Let's do something about it soon," he said. "I've tried hard with your father, but we need to move forward."

"Well, Mr. Holly," Jess said with feigned surprise and a Scarlett O'Hara delivery. "Is that a proposal of marriage?"

"Frankly, my dear, I suppose that's pretty close. But right now, coffee calls." Jake rose from the bed. "By the way," he said as he departed the room. "Who were you thinking should bear my children?"

"You'll pay for that!" she yelled, laughing and hurling a pillow at the doorway.

Jake hustled through his morning ablutions. Within fifteen minutes he was shaved and showered and standing in the kitchen layering nine-grain toast with unsalted Irish butter and wild plum jelly. The coffee beans were ground and being showered with scalding water in the Krups. A lump of Black Diamond cheddar and two crisp Fuji apples sat on the cutting board. Like the rest of his house, Jake's kitchen was saturated with contemporary sleekness clothed in an antique shell. When he bought the property after fleeing Missouri, it was a thistly twenty-eight acres with an octogenarian farmhouse in poor repair. Jake transformed the acreage, the house, and himself. He did much of the work alone and in silence, as if he were a medieval monk, mourning Allie every minute of every day.

He started a two-acre garden of baby vegetables, declining to bathe them in pesticides and learning the hard way the bugs would reap his harvest. Making a living wasn't an issue. After selling the Live Right Express locations to a large company intent on expansion, plus Allie's life insurance, which the bank had required, Jake was financially fixed for life. Still, he needed to believe in what he was trying to do. A few days in Portland and Seattle selling what the bugs overlooked convinced Jake there was a growing market for organic baby vegetables. Fine-dining chefs in both cities wanted whatever he could bring them, regardless of price—within reason. Basically they committed to buying all the carrots, potatoes, lettuces, asparagus, zucchini, celery, and heirloom tomatoes Jake could grow, plus nearly anything else "baby" and "organic" he wanted to try.

"Don't worry," one of the chefs told him, "this stuff will fly off the menu. This is how people want to eat, and our customers are willing to pay for it."

The second year, Jake learned to battle the bugs without resorting to chemistry. He planted nearly five acres and made sure everything that grew was strong. Regular watering, aerating, and weeding made for strong cell walls in the plants. Around certain varieties, he recycled plastic, one-liter bottles into a barrier two inches into the ground to protect from cutworms and other soil dwellers. He walked the gardens constantly and removed bugs by hand, dropping them into a bottle of soapy water.

Then he called in the good guys. He planted borders of mint, clover, thyme, and fennel so there would be an abundance of flowers for the beneficial insects. Soon he had a crop of lacewings, assassin bugs, ground beetles, praying mantis, and ladybugs to gobble the aphids and other pests. He flooded a low area to make dragonfly heaven. The bluebirds, purple martins, and bats nearby were quick to pitch in, keeping the farm mosquito-free, though they were also prone to snag a dragonfly when they could catch one.

By the third year, the acreage was in balance and productive. Jake hired a foreman, along with several seasonal workers and a twice-a-week delivery driver to cover both Portland and Seattle in a shiny, new Mercedes box truck. Jake called his business The Provisioner. His logo featured a clump of baby carrots with a smiling ladybug. By plowing the profits back into the land, Jake planted several acres of orchard trees and berry bushes. He hoped the current year would bring fragrant peaches and a few hazelnuts. Next year, maybe blackberries and raspberries. Lately, he'd given some thought to grapes and wine.

"Hey, Scarlett," Jake called to Jess. "Are you dressed yet? It's time to call your dad."

"Two more minutes," she called back. "I need extra makeup today. I'm still blushing from last night."

Jake looked her over admiringly when she breezed into the kitchen four minutes later. He handed her a coffee and a slab of toast. She took a hungry bite and gave it the "mmmmm" seal of approval. They sat down at the table.

"Are you OK with calling him this early?"

"Yep. I know he'll be up and about. What did we decide I'm going to say?"

"As little as possible. Just ask him to meet us at Swampy's about seven fifteen or seven thirty. Convince him that it's important and he needs to trust you. If you have to start explaining, it's going to get complicated. We can get there before he does and lead him inside for show-and-tell. OK?"

"Sure. So after we get there, will you do the talking?"

"I'll tell him exactly what happened and ask his advice on how to proceed. Hopefully, he'll become the public spokesman. We'll go through a few days of media blitz and then the anthropologists will haul her off and take over. Splitty and I will have to stay out of the woods for a while. There'll be a lot of wannabes out there when this gets out."

"You say, 'for a while.' Does that mean you'll go back out there, knowing they exist?"

"I might be a little skittish at first. But I doubt I'll ever see another Sasquatch. This was the perfect storm. Pardon the expression."

Jessica took her coffee and cell phone for a walk. Jake could hear her talking, but couldn't make out the words. When she returned to the kitchen, she started tidying up and said, "All set. He didn't ask for any explanation, just wanted to make sure you were coming."

They took the last of their coffee to the screened porch off the master bedroom. The morning was clear and moist. Taking a deep breath was like having dessert. The promise of spring hung pregnantly in the intoxicating air. Bumblebees buzzed at the clumps of purple wisteria flowers climbing the porch corners. A fat deerfly executed a kamikaze dive against the screen wire and made a metallic clunk. He fell to the ledge below, regaining composure only after a series of silent wing ruffles. For a moment the only sound was a susurrus of breeze sighing through the screen and a distant mockingbird welcoming the day with his repertoire of song.

"I hate to say it, but this morning feels like the eye of a hurricane," Jake said. "At least to me."

"Oh, I was thinking of something else, my dear Mr. Holly. I was thinking about the lovely things you said about children. Listen please, Jacob. You're a very good man, probably in more ways than you realize. I love you. I know you're fretting terribly because you killed that creature, but sometimes things just happen. Even to good people. It could have happened to someone else, but it didn't. You did the right thing and brought her in. This day will pass, and the next one, and the next, and the next. We'll be fine, whatever comes."

Jake leaned close and kissed her neck twice. "I'm glad you're here."

"Well said, homeboy. Think about it. There are billions of folks out there who will spend today talking about septic tanks or what they want for lunch. We won't be among them. We'll be talking about a humongous scientific discovery."

He kissed her ear and bit it gently. She turned with purpose and kissed him hungrily on the mouth and nibbled his lower lip playfully.

"Did you say, 'I love you,' in there somewhere?" Jake asked.

"I did. But you've heard that before. You said today felt like calm before the storm, and I sense that too. But you know what feels different about this morning? I don't feel Allie with us. I've never wanted you to forget her, and I know you won't. One thing that makes me love you is the way you honor her six years after she died. Don't stop doing that. You can hold her memory and still let her go. You'll have plenty of love left over for me."

Jake turned serious. "You make it easy. You're a singular commodity." He held her at arm's length. "Listen to me, madam counselor. I love you too, with every shred of my existence. I wake up every morning and think how lucky I am. Love is what's left after falling in love is over. There's a lot left over. You were channeling Scarlett and asking if I was proposing. I'm thinking it's time. Nobody wishes for happiness at a later date."

Jess was glued to Jake's eyes. She squeezed his hands and said, "Thank you, Jacob. That was beautiful. Obviously, I'm as ready as you are to move forward. Let's get this piddling little Bigfoot issue handled and see what comes next, OK?"

"Fair enough." He looked at her with the faintest of subservience. He was addressing Helen of Troy. "My, my," he said. "Did something just happen? Did a wind blow through? OK by me. Let's get to Oscar's before the others. You ready?"

9

OSCAR'S 2—THE MORNING SURPRISE

A surprise was waiting at the rear of the Marsh Funeral Home at 6:57 a.m. Two occupied cars were parked and waiting. One belonged to Jess's dad, the other to the county sheriff.

"Why do you suppose he's already here? And why on earth would he bring the sheriff?"

"I don't have a clue. He didn't say anything on the phone. Just said he would be here."

They parked and got out. Sheriff Eldo Throckmorton exited his squad car and approached. Eldo usually displayed to the world an easy smile, but this time his demeanor was serious. A wag at Hee-Haw's once said Mother Nature intended to make an oak tree, but changed her mind at the last minute and made Eldo instead. An ex-Navy SEAL and Vietnam veteran, Eldo kept his six-foot, four-inch frame in muscular shape, had arms the size of legs, and wore outdated sideburns with a droopy, salt-and-pepper mustache. He possessed piercing brown eyes that looked like they could bend a spoon at twenty paces. He walked straight to Jake.

"Morning, Jake."

"Hey, Eldo. You're out early this morning."

"Jake, I'm here because I was asked to be here. I want you to know that. Talburt called me late last night, and he runs the show." Eldo lifted his head and pointed his chin at Jake. "Jake, by order of the county prosecuting attorney, I'm placing you under arrest. You have the right to remain—"

"Eldo, what's going on? What are you arresting me for?"

"I'm sorry, Jake. Like I said, I'm following orders. You're being arrested for murder. You're under arrest for murder."

Jake shook his head and looked toward Tal. "I can tell you're not kidding, Eldo. What the hell is going on here?"

"Talburt calls the shots. He says you killed something, and it's human enough that he's doing this. I won't handcuff you if you promise to do what I ask. Deal?"

"Yes, deal. I'm not going anywhere, and this is completely nuts."

Jessica was standing to the side, turning red and watching in shock. Tal urged his daughter to the front bumper with a backward tilt of his head just as Oscar drove up and parked. "What's going on here, Dad?" Her voice cracked and rose. She was trying, but failing, to sound calm. Her voice betrayed her rising anger. "Jake, come over here. Dad, I asked you a simple question. What are you doing? You can't be serious about this."

Jake took a position beside Jessica. Eldo came a step behind. Tal held up a hand as if to articulate something.

Oscar joined the group, smiled, and repeated Jess's question. "What's going on? Why the long faces?"

"Now hold on a minute," Tal said. "Everyone take a deep breath and let me try to explain myself." He cleared his throat. "Jessica, when you called me this morning, I already knew what it was about. I was glad you called. You and Jake wanting to meet me here makes it clear nobody's trying to hide anything. I assume you shot that creature lying inside, Jake. Is that right?"

"That's right, Tal. It was an accident. How can you already know about this? Have you seen her?"

"I have. Last night I got a call from Rod Wooten, and he told me a wild story. His boy Chuckie and Ed Lasswell's boy Billy are pals, and the Lasswell boy had come running to Rod's house with a tale about seeing someone unload a huge dead thing into Oscar's place here. He claimed a Bigfoot grabbed him up and set him down right over there across the street. He described you and Jessica and your pickup.

"I guess you can imagine I didn't believe a word of what Rod was telling me. Neither did Rod. He called because he didn't know what else to do. At first, I was going to ignore it and go to bed, but then I remembered Eldo had a set of keys to Oscar's, like he does for many of the businesses around town in case of fire or burglary or something. Completely voluntary. I got hold of Eldo and he met me here. We found her in the cold room. If that thing's not damn near human, then I don't know a cow patty from a turnip."

"But, Dad—" Jess started.

Ignoring her, Tal continued, "Jake, you claim it was an accident. I heard that. But she's been shot right through the head. That took pretty good aim. I know a little something about your habits and your rides out there in the tall trees. I know you carry a loaded weapon with you. Hell, I sure don't blame you for that. A man can run into some things out there. Anyone who's ever hunted knows a loaded weapon wants to be fired and might even want to go off on its own. But it can't. Somebody has to gather up the momentum and pull the trigger. That had to be you."

Jake stared at Tal, wondering how things got so out of control.

"Seems like you've answered the question of whether or not ol' Sasquatch exists," Tal acknowledged. "That's what she is, lying in there on Oscar's table, right? That'll take a lot of starch out of the disbelievers, won't it? You and I both know the zoologists and hunters have been arguing for years about whether someone ought to shoot one if they had the chance. Some thought it would be murder; some thought the scientific value would justify it. Then you get into the ethics and morality. Jake, I'm pretty sure you know some of these discussions favored Sasquatch being declared an endangered species and shooting one to be a felony. There are just too many points of view for me to ignore what's happened. I have to do something, don't you see? That thing lying on the slab is terribly human looking. Not long ago, a court in New York State was asked to rule on whether or not chimpanzees were entitled to 'legal personhood,' for Pete's sake. It's my job to do something."

"Dad, that's a total crock," Jessica interrupted. She no longer tried to hide her irritation. "This is about Jake and me, and you're trying—"

"Jessica Ruth, I am not finished," Talburt shot back. "Now, the law defines murder as the unlawful killing of one human being by another. It's not up to me to say what kind of being that creature is. That's for the scientists to decide. But for my money, she's more human than anything else that comes to mind. That's why Eldo is arresting you, Jake. The other thing is this. The Lasswell and Wooten boys have already spread this all over the Internet and called everyone they could think of. I figure we've got about a day or two before our little Aurora becomes the center of the universe. We'd better have our ducks in a row. Eldo and I are already swamped with messages from folks wanting to know what's going on, and it's barely seven o'clock on a Saturday morning. A lot of people don't work today, so this is what they'll be fussing about, whether there's any truth to what they're hearing. The Lasswell boy claims something snatched him up when he was here last night. That seemed like a wild-eyed kid story at first, but knowing what's inside . . . maybe the boy is telling the truth. Did you see another one, Jake?"

"Mr. O'Reilly," Jake said, looking him directly in the eye, "I'm trying to understand why you're doing this. I hope it's not what Jess was saying, some kind of vendetta."

"Not at all," Tal insisted, almost convincingly. "I tried to explain."

Jake continued. "Yes, there were two of them, a male and a female. I told you it was a complete accident. They were suddenly in front of me and I was dozing in a tree cutout during the storm. I shoved the rifle at them and it went off. It seemed like it went off by itself, but I must have pulled the trigger. I didn't know I was pulling it. My heart was in my throat and I wasn't quite awake."

"What did the male do?"

"The slug went through his shoulder and hit the female in the head. His arm was injured, but he just about knocked me down with his bellowing. He tried to pick her up. When he couldn't, he eventually left. And I brought her in."

"That must have taken some doing, Jake. OK. Let's you and Eldo and I go down to the courthouse and write up a full statement. We'll release you on your own recognizance, but I've got to do this. I've got to do something. If this isn't a mess, it'll have to do until one comes along. Oscar, you haven't said a word. Sorry about all this. You know we wouldn't have used the key if it weren't important. Have you got a good padlock to lock up that cold room?"

Oscar had assumed the time-honored pose of the funeral director, well postured with arms in front, crossed at the wrist. "Yes, I can lock it up," he said without emotion.

"Then please do so, if you will. I'm leaving you out of this. I'd appreciate if you'd make sure no one else sees it or hears anything until we decide what to do. OK?"

"Fine."

"Thank you. Eldo, Jake, let's roll."

The three men covered the six steps to Eldo's squad car. Tal opened the door to his own vehicle before he noticed his daughter climbing into the sheriff's back seat with Jake.

"What are you doing, Jessica?" Tal asked. "Don't you want to bring Jake's pickup?"

"No can do, Mr. Prosecuting Attorney," she said with icicles dripping. She stood outside the vehicle. Her face was ashen. She spoke in a cutting tone draped with irony. Her eyes narrowed but did not blink. "I helped bring the body in and hide it. That makes me an accessory to your so-called murder. Anybody who watches TV could tell you that, and need I remind you that I'm also an attorney? You book him, you book me." She ducked into the cruiser and reached for Jake's hand. "Let's go," she said.

10

TOKYO REPORTER KENZO

Kenzo Matsuki was the chief investigative reporter for a leading Japanese newspaper, the *Morning Star*. As Jessica slammed the door to Eldo Throckmorton's cruiser at 7:07 a.m. Saturday in Washington State, Kenzo was checking his laptop at nearly midnight Saturday evening in Tokyo on his way to bed. He was equipped with software that combed the Internet around the planet for all things unusual, things he might turn into interesting copy for his newspaper. Mostly, it was a waste of time that entailed lots of deleting. He zapped the usual barrage of breathless but delusive claims from the swamp of human flotsam—alien abductions, outrageous crimes, corruption, pornography—delete, delete, delete. But something from an obscure chat room called "weirdbumpinthenight" caught his attention. An American boy was blogging about a Sasquatch encounter he claimed to have experienced. His web handle was "billwell." The earnest tone of the writer, who said he was twelve, stopped Kenzo's click on the Delete button. His finger froze on the mouse as he read:

> the thing looked me right in the eye
> it shook its head from side to side

i thought it was going to throw me down and hurt me
i was very scared
then it was like it looked close at me and it was dark
but its face looked human
the rest of it was so big i can't even tell you
it had to be ten feet tall like a basketball goal
then it put me down and i ran and ran

Someone called AshokM wrote: "they always say Bigfoot smells bad—did it stink?"

Billwell replied: "i don't think so / it was kind of raining most of the time / i didn't smell anything bad."

Kenzo leaned back and pondered the tone of the exchange. He read English much better than he spoke it. He logged quickly into the chat room and began to ask questions himself. He had an urge to find out where the boy was located and why he would tell a preposterous story about a Bigfoot corpse and close encounter.

11

WASHINGTON, DC, REPORTER DAVE

Dave Hulett came by his position at *U.S. News & World Report* the old-fashioned way. He inherited it. His father, Swann, had attended the University of Missouri School of Journalism in Columbia and worked his way up the ranks of big-time reporting. Thanks in part to an exclusive and controversial interview with his former college roommate, who was chief of staff to the president of the United States, Swann was made executive editor of the prestigious news magazine, which was trying to become a believable and professional online presence. Dave followed in his father's footsteps, both at Mizzou and with his staff assignment at *U.S. News.* But he wasn't a legacy without ambition and talent of his own.

In his year and a half back in DC and on the magazine's staff, his job had largely been confined to rewriting the reporting of others. He did it with verve and a knack for wordsmithing, but he was sick of it. Dave didn't live a day without imagining that he was destined to uncover a defining scoop and bring glory to himself and the magazine. At age thirty, he was not disposed to a slow climb up the ladder. He needed the big story, and the sooner the better.

By midmorning that Saturday, Dave had consumed four cups of strong coffee and five newspapers. In his e-mail inbox, he found a compelling note from a college buddy, a graduate teaching assistant who spent ten hours a day online. The note guided Dave to the weirdbumpinthenight chat room and other linked sites abuzz with Bigfootiana. In the space of a few hours, rumor, one-upmanship, creativity, and pure bunkum were growing exponentially. In some of the chat, Billy Lasswell's tale deformed into alien abduction. In another version, the government appropriated the Bigfoot body and hid it away. One hyperactive blogger claimed that while the entire incident was true, the creature wasn't a Bigfoot but the result of military experiments to create an army of mutants with superhuman size and strength. A writer with tongue firmly in cheek suggested the huge, hairy corpse was actually a guy who rubbed penis-enlargement cream over his entire body.

Dave spent a good hour working from site to site and watching the tale grow taller and taller, then returned to the simple, nearly emotionless chat-room entries of billwell. Eventually, he rose from his computer and found his wife making a bed. He explained that it was probably a wild-goose chase and that he had tried unsuccessfully to phone public officials in Aurora, Washington, but he was thinking seriously of going there mmediately.

After a quick call to his father, Dave had the green light. He rose from his desk, packed in ten minutes, and stepped into an Uber with his overnight bag. He was on his cell making reservations, headed to Ronald Reagan Airport. Had it not been the weekend, Dave would have been working on other people's copy. There would have been little time to fuss with the Internet and depart on a long shot. But he had a reporter's instinct and plenty of optimism that a cross-country trip chasing a Bigfoot shooting would make an interesting feature story, even when the shooting turned out to be bogus.

12

NEW DELHI REPORTER ASHOK

Ashok Mahadevan would have been royalty a century ago. His family had a long and princely history in India. His great-grandfather had been a maharaja, and only during his grandfather's time had the family's land holdings been usurped by revisionist regimes spawned by the never-ending Muslim-Hindu conflicts. His veins still ran with blue blood in the Indian way of seeing things, but Ashok chose a different path. Instead of hanging loose in his father's deteriorating mini palace with its dozen servants, Ashok was a bachelor workingman. As a reporter for the *Delhi Mail*, he was a Brahman with no qualms about walking the streets of New Delhi with untouchables. While online and questioning "billwell" about the smell of Bigfoot, he was working a computer network that was part of his night job. Besides being a part-time reporter, he was a customer service rep for Delhi Tigers Inc., an outsourcing haven for dozens of US companies, including several from the Fortune 500.

Ashok's interest in the Sasquatch chatter at weirdbumpinthenight, a site he visited regularly, was consistent with his basic instinct as a conspiracy theorist par excellence. He was the author of three books in Hindi—one on the JFK assassination, one debating whether or not astronauts actually went to the moon, and his most recent, a series of interviews with Himalayan tribesmen who claimed to have seen the Abominable Snowman. The books generated a small but profitable following. They were quickly translated into Punjabi, Bengali, and English.

Ashok was about to begin a week's paid vacation from Delhi Tigers after his shift. He sent a text his newspaper editor that he was chasing a story. Within two hours of deciding that a Sasquatch book would complement his publishing portfolio, Ashok was boarding a flight to Tokyo. There was a good connection from Tokyo to San Francisco, and he reasoned there would be a bus or train to the Aurora, Washington, area and it couldn't be that far from San Francisco. Ashok was fuzzy on US geography and short on his estimate of time and distance, but he was long on curiosity and testosterone.

13

SPIT HITS FAN AT WHITE HOUSE

Swann Hulett paused a full minute after hanging up with his son, Dave. He closed his eyes and ran his tongue over his teeth as he pondered his next step. Deliberately, he pecked out the secret cell number of the president's chief of staff. Only two journalists had the number for Stanton Buckley. The other was managing editor of the *Washington Post*. Buckley's aide answered on the first ring.

"Staff office. Who's calling, please?"

"Hi, Ed. This is Swann Hulett. You guys are plugging away on the weekend, huh?"

"Hey, Swann. You got that right. What's a weekend? You know we don't get time off like you civilians. What can I do for you? It must be a big story you're chasing if you're calling this number. Nobody uses this number."

"I know, Ed. My apologies for the interruption. Actually, I'm not chasing a story at all. This is more like doing my duty. I need to talk to Stan for a minute. There's something I think the president should be aware of. Could you please have Stan call me back on a secure line? I'm at my home. He's got the number."

"I'll be glad to pass it along. He's got a couple of senators buttonholing him right now. Give him a little bit."

"Great. Thanks for your help."

"No problem. Our guys appreciate the way you handle a tough job. Most of the time, you try to be fair with the administration."

"Balance, my boy, balance. Evenhandedness is a scarce commodity in journalism today, but I'm kind of a dinosaur. Thanks again. Hope I run into you sometime soon."

"Take care, Swann."

———— ✦ ————

Minutes later, the call came through. "Hello, Swann. How you doing? Haven't seen you for a while."

"Thanks for returning the call, Stan. Sorry to interrupt. I wouldn't have used your private number—except I might have something kind of urgent if there's any truth to it. I hope you're not in the middle of a crisis."

"That's why you have the number, besides being my old roomie. I appreciate the job you do, and I think it's mutually beneficial for you to reach out if you think it's justified. No, we're not having a bad day. Just the usual BS trying to convince a gaggle of senators to line up with us. What's on your mind?"

"I know this will sound a little odd. Maybe a lot odd. And I know your job description doesn't include little green men and big hairy monsters. But my son is on his way to Washington State, and he's convinced something unusual is going down. Dave can be gullible and overly ambitious at times, but he usually doesn't go off half-cocked. He thinks somebody up in the north woods shot a Sasquatch and some kid saw the body. I thought you and POTUS would want a heads-up."

"Hold on a sec, Swann. Did you say *shot a Sasquatch*? Is it dead?"

"I wish I knew the details. Most of Dave's information is coming from the Internet, so God knows if there's any truth to it. He thinks the chase will make a good story even if it's hogwash. I thought about letting him go and not calling you until I knew more, but if Dave's leaving his family on a weekend to fly cross-country, something has convinced him. If even a speck of it is authentic, I know the government wants to be involved as soon as possible."

"Agreed," Stanton said, motioning an aide closer. "It sounds like we need to look into it right away. Tell me what you know and what you want from me. I'll inform POTUS as soon as we hang up."

14

THE EERIE DARK DIVIDE

North and east of Aurora runs a ridge that divides the watershed between the Cispus and Lewis Rivers. It's a wild and complex and roadless area known as the Dark Divide, part of Gifford Pinchot National Forest. Though most Aurorians would say it's named after the mysterious light that slants through its giant and ancient trees or the dark basalt formations that jut from its rich soil, they would be mistaken. The name derives, less satisfyingly, from an early miner named John Dark.

The swirling mass of tall trees is the primary foundation for this complex and superhuman-sized country, but it's the random and fabulous mess of fallen trees that make the ground nearly impassable. The huge, mossy, pungent logs are strewn through the forest as if the gods were playing pickup sticks. Visibility is foreshortened to the distance between dark shadows and dappled piles of wood. Forest researchers studying the profound fertility of the treescapes of western North America have discovered a complex web of fungi in the soil the big trees grow in, a web that links many of the tree species and provides them an avenue to each other very much like communication. This phenomenon has been dubbed the Wood Wide Web. In this remarkable synergy, the trees exchange carbon back and forth and help each other be more robust, depending on the season.

Here and there a peek of deciduous hardwood provides a variation on the theme of green. Concentrate on the horizon and a view of the mountains rising up to kiss the clouds may emerge. The ground is perpetually damp as the giant trees drip water from rain and humidity. The air is likewise moist and fresh-smelling. To the south lie the gently rolling hills of the Willamette River valley, the Columbia River bluffs, the cities of northwestern Oregon, all bustling with the urgent activities of humanity. But north of the Columbia, the big pines take over the landscape, jutting their Christmas tree tops into the deep slate sky. It's a land of contrasts, this quadrant of America, dotted with sea-level lakes and busy rivers and aspiring mountains and impossible forests, the whole of it a complicated confluence of human habitation and natural wonder.

Is there forensic evidence of Bigfoot in the Dark Divide? There are footprints and alleged sightings, of course, and anecdotal reports of close encounters. But most of the evidence wouldn't be admissible in court. There are rumors and whispers and I'd-rather-not-talk-about-it utterances from forest wayfarers who then proceed to talk about it at length, indulging the human yearning for monsters. There are insinuations and leaks from credible persons who will only confess their brush with Bigfoot if granted anonymity, and not-so-credible braggadocio from those who cloak themselves in Sasquatchiana. There is the Native American population's abandonment of areas considered too dangerous because of the monster's proximity, and Indian children keeping a nervous watch while berry picking. There is the logical cleft stick that if Sasquatch is nothing more than legend, a considerable body of circumstantial evidence and reliable sightings must be explained away. That such creatures once existed is beyond dispute. Therefore, there is the simple logic that if large, hairy, humanlike creatures still exist, that if such a thing is real, it should, it must, live among the Pacific Northwest's impossibly grand forests.

15

SECRETS OF THE CAVE

The creatures had used tools for millennia. In their powerful hands a sharp-edged limb became a drill bit, a slab of tough bark transformed into a shovel. They often carried such tools on hunting and foraging expeditions. One of their hunting techniques—the simple digging of a camouflaged hole for a trap—sometimes proved useful in avoiding discovery by humans walking the trails. As a last resort when contact seemed unavoidable, they could dig a shallow hole among heavy brush, lie down, and cover up in half a minute.

Through the generations, they passed down the attribute to move quietly and remain hidden in the woods, even when sometimes very close to humans. It was an ability that deer and other prey animals often discovered the hard way. The fittest and best-fed Sasquatch survived to pass along their stealthy traits to offspring, a highly useful permutation through the centuries. Though they didn't mind sleeping in the open, caves were home. There were many to choose from in the wild and mountainous terrain. The preferred caves were well away from human activity with hidden entrances, some not more than a crack in the earth to squeeze through. All the better if the crack appeared to lead nowhere but opened up inside. Best of all was the Cascades' mother cave, which was about fifteen miles from Aurora.

The area around the entrance had every advantage a Bigfoot's instinct could desire. Halfway up a remote mountaintop, loose soil disappeared and rock outcroppings offered places to walk that left no tracks. The mother cave was just below the tree line and therefore covered by shortish trees and gnarly brush that could have flourished in solid concrete, if given time. Wild berries abounded. Salmonberry, cloudberry, and saskatoon cohabited with stunted red alders and big-leaf maples to provide flawless cover for the cave entrance, which was little more than a dark fissure in a flinty hillside. Over the past two hundred years of white human intrusion and the preceding millennia of tribal presence, the cave entrance had been noticed, rarely, by Klickitats and Yakimas, mountain men, surveying loggers, and even the odd hiker or two. The entrance had been breached on rare occasions by curious humans who were disappointed to discover that just inside, the cave seemed to end in a forty-foot rock wall.

Had these inquisitive souls been able to scale the steep wall in the dark, like the Sasquatch could, had they brought along a strong light and stronger resolve, they might have discovered the setback opening above the wall that led to hundreds of yards of passages and many large rooms beyond. There were even tiny cracks in the stone ceiling that allowed the faintest light to penetrate the passageways, along with an occasional drip of water to use as a drinking fountain. Outside the hidden cave entrance, when the loaded berry bushes semaphored ripeness with their bright colors and treacly smell, energetic birds arrived in an army of appetite. Mid-mountain late summer became an Eden swarming with flycatchers, ravens, chickadees, jays, and juncos, plus the ravenous bears trying to bloat themselves—as long as they didn't sense a Bigfoot. When they did, they departed in an urgent lope and made low, huffing noises. Bears avoided confrontation with Bigfoot.

Most Sasquatch were part of a family unit similar to their human cousins. An extended family might forage together late in the day and into the night, then lie down together to sleep. Serious hunting was done after dark by the alpha males, who brought venison, feral pork, and fish to the collective. The males provided for and mated with two or three females, who yielded rich milk and tender care for the offspring. Females usually gave birth to a single baby, but fraternal twins weren't uncommon. Aging uncles and aunts were accepted into the families when they were beyond mating. They rendered attentive babysitting and sentry duty. The creatures could live to an old age well past fifty.

Theorists on the development of human consciousness have suggested that in prehistoric times, our hominid ancestors had bicameral minds to facilitate the demands of survival. They could pigeonhole important instincts into a sharply divided, dual brain. One side of the brain could talk to the other side, according to these theories, even issuing God-like commands that actually originated in the individual. A useful schizophrenia may have prevailed in prehumans. As the two sides of the brain evolved to become integrated, these theories propose, thinking became unicameral and permitted human self-consciousness to arise. The endless interior monologue began. As for the northwestern Sasquatch, despite their stunted evolutionary path, the merging was evident. Away from the chores of hunting and gathering in secret, they were capable of being pensive.

On a Saturday morning in May, if a lucky anthropologist had been kneeling on the hill above the mother cave and threading a tiny, infrared camera into a crack in the rock, down, down, two hundred feet below into the void, he might have threaded into the main cavern and seen a sight to make his heart race. He might first have seen faintly glowing logs in a depression on the cave floor. In the dim light, he might have seen Sasquatch, twenty-three in total, divided into several families and of varying sizes and ages, in a rough circle around the logs. He might have fiddled with a knob on his headset and cocked his head downward and cupped his hand over one ear to block the soft wind, then listened so intently that a bear could have walked up on him. He might have heard things—rustling noises and low mutters, and taken them for nothing more than the cave, sighing and breathing. Then, however, he might have realized the sounds were coming from the Sasquatch, bent low to the cave floor. He might have recognized the sounds of vowels and clicks and rudimentary words. *Gaa. Uuuta. Kooee. Ooteek.* There was no lucky anthropologist, of course, no headset or camera, no bear. There was only the misty sunshine and the spring zephyr and the berry buds and the smoke and steam to the west from an awakened volcano—and twenty-three Sasquatch kneeling in a cave, looking as if they might be praying.

16

FIRST MEETING—JESS AND JAKE

They met in the produce aisle of a grocery store.

She spoke first. "I don't believe I've ever seen a man looking closely at an eggplant."

He turned and looked for the first time into her striking face. The timing was right. He smiled and said, "Hello. Did you ever wonder how anything that looks so beautiful can be so tasteless? I was thinking if you grew them small and maybe crossed with garlic, they'd be better."

"But would they still be eggplant?" Jessica said. "Some things are prized specifically because they don't have a strong flavor of their own. The cook can season them to taste. Veal is a good example. Why else would we pen up baby cows and slaughter them when they're young? Eggplant is the same. You have to meet it halfway. Do it in good olive oil with cheese and tomatoes and you've got something."

"Good point," Jake said. "But if you put olive oil and cheese and tomatoes on tree bark, it wouldn't be bad." His smile grew wider and his eyes signaled mischief. "But we shouldn't debate eggplant without knowing names. I'm

Jake Holly. I haven't lived here too long. I'm re-doing the old Wolfinbarger place west of town."

"Hello, Jake Holly. I'm Jessica O'Reilly, and I'm about as local as you can get. I was born and raised here except for college and law school. I've lived here all my life. My dad is Tal O'Reilly, the county prosecuting attorney."

"Oh, sure. Everybody's heard of him. Actually, I've lived here more than two years now. I keep a low profile."

"And I've heard of you. Local buzz has you pegged as a mystery man. Moved here by yourself from the Midwest, and being a hermit out there on your property. Rumor has it you might be in witness protection. You seem normal to me, except for your eggplant fetish."

Jake laughed out loud and moved closer to her in the supermarket aisle. He looked directly into her brownish-green eyes and liked what he saw. Something stirred in him, something he hadn't felt for a long time. He'd had almost no contact with the opposite sex since Allie died nearly six years earlier. He knew it would not be easy to talk to another woman, to get used to a stranger's ways and habits. But instinctively, perhaps out of self-preservation, he knew he should try. "Look," he said, "tell me if I'm out of line. You know nothing about me and I know nothing about you— except that you're bright and beautiful. That's not bad for starters. Maybe you've got a husband and six kids, but would you like to go for a cup of coffee with no strings attached?"

It was Jessica's turn to smile. "Thank you for the compliment. No weirdo hermit could have said such nice things. Nope—no husband, no kids. Plenty of dating, but not lately. I'd be pleased to have coffee with you, Mr. Jake

Holly, if you're through shopping. Let's go across the street to Hee-Haw's. He actually makes decent coffee this time of day."

"If I weren't through shopping, I am now. Lead the way."

At Hee-Haw's they slipped comfortably into what would become their favorite booth. The icebreaker conversation might have been trivial, but it wasn't. Both were able to talk comfortably about a wide range of topics. The attraction was immediate. In the months and years to come, they would find refuge in each other and a tolerance for each other's imperfections that would make life an easier proposition. When black clouds arose and reminded them of their frailty, calm would follow the storm.

"So, you mentioned law school. I guess that means you're a lawyer?" Jake was enjoying looking intently into her eyes.

"Hey, you were actually listening," Jess said. "You get a gold star. Yes, it's true. I didn't expect it, but like Daddy, I'm a lawyer. Except he's in the business of putting people in jail, and I'm usually trying to keep them out. My firm defends the accused. Aurora is small, but things still happen, especially with the drug scene. We cover eight counties, and sometimes we get people who can't afford a lawyer but surely need one. We try to take those cases too."

"You speak of your father like he's your opponent. Do you get along with him?"

"Sure. Absolutely. We get along fine. He's always thought of me as a daddy's girl and he's probably right. We butt heads in court and then have lunch. It's just that he casts a long shadow around here. Hey, enough about me. Where did you come from and what are you doing to that house and land you bought?"

Jake was still looking at her eyes. "No, no, not so fast. We'll go there in a minute. Now start at the beginning and go straight through, family skeletons and all. You were born here. What were you like in the first grade?"

Jess leaned back and turned loose an uninhibited cackle that startled Jake for a moment, though he would come to love that laugh.

"First grade?" she said. "You're serious, aren't you? OK. I'll do that. But when it's your turn, it's the same deal, first grade."

Jake couldn't hold back a smirk as he said, "Fine with me. I guess in first grade you were all fat and ugly and dumb."

She smirked back. "What? No way, Jake Holly. I looked like Shirley Temple and ciphered like Archimedes. . . ."

She talked about grade school in Aurora, where the strict teachers took no guff and force-fed the basics. She talked about her family, about growing up the youngest of three and therefore having to work hard to keep up. She talked about Louise, her father's sister, and the marital problems she'd endured. Jake was spellbound by it all. His steady gaze kept her talking right through high school and beyond until he had a genuine feel for this altogether pleasant woman.

"So now you're a successful lawyer with a booming practice," Jake said. "But you left out one thing. Why aren't you married? None of my business, but I can't help asking."

"Ask away. I don't mind. Sure, I've had offers. My mother convinced me not to rush into it, and I learned she was right. After some time goes by, suddenly there are issues. Always issues. If you want someone to stay the same, they change. If you want someone to change a little, they stay the same. The problem is how do you keep the passion alive? Something about relationships makes them deteriorate over time. Maybe familiarity does breed contempt. Absence makes the heart grow fonder and all that. When you think about it, 'till death do us part' started back when life expectancy was about thirty years. Good grief, now we live three times that long—and we have many more years to annoy each other. They say it just takes a lot of hard work."

"I appreciate the candor," Jake said. "You've obviously given this a lot of thought. Normally I'm not much of a coffee drinker, but this is the best thing that's happened to me lately."

Jess leaned forward in anticipation. "OK, your turn. And remember the rules."

"I was afraid you'd say that." Jake gave Hee-Haw's simple brew an unnecessary stir as he thought how to begin. The basic coffee was advertised by a sign above the bar: *No latte. No espresso. No cappuccino. Coffee.*

"I became a widower at thirty-five, six years or so ago. My wife's name was Allie. We were married for eight years, and most of it was good. Not every day was a holiday, of course, but if a man and woman can board the same train, they can manage being together. You just can't expect more than is possible."

"So there's a reason for the isolation," Jess said. "I expected as much. But don't forget to start in the first grade. You probably had no front teeth and a cowlick." She tapped her forefinger on the table for emphasis and gave Jake an exaggerated appraisal. She was attracted to his athletic maleness and didn't bother to hide it. He liked that she easily matched his needling banter.

"All right, all right, first grade. I could run like a deer and had the attention span of a ferret. Maybe a ferret drinking Hee-Haw's coffee. In grade school my report cards were fine, but they always had that teacher note about not working hard enough to realize potential.

"The town in Missouri had a nice little creek running through it and was semifamous for albino squirrels. We always lived in town, but I admired the farm boys. They knew a lot about the real world. When I was around eight, this guy who worked in the local drugstore took perverse delight in telling me about the grandmother I never met. My folks said they intended to tell me when I was old enough, but hadn't gotten around to it. I felt like everyone knew except me. My grandfather had been a big shot and established a chain of grocery stores called Pennysavers in several small towns in the area. This was long before anyone ever heard of chain markets. They had a big house and a young, single woman as a maid. There was small-town jealousy over his success— especially over the maid since she was the only one in town. Sometimes people in small towns are especially pleasant and sometimes they're just small. So the rumor got started that my grandfather was friendlier with the maid than he was supposed to be. He was a fairly young man at that time. Whether it was true or not, nobody knows, but a lot of people believed it. My grandmother was this frail, little woman to begin with, and the rumor was hard for her to deal with. She had headaches and was bedridden for days at a time. One day after a big rain, the creek was swollen with rolling water. Grandmother went for a walk and didn't come back. They found her body caught up in a tangle of branches downstream and had a heck of a time recovering her. Half the locals, including Granddad, were on the bank of the creek when they finally got a hook on her and pulled her out. Immediately, some of the smallest of the small decided she'd jumped into the water and that Granddad and the maid might as well have pushed her. They found her footprints on the muddy bank where she went in. Some thought it looked like she fell; others thought she jumped. She was only forty-one years old. My mother was seven or eight. The local newspaper carried it on the front page under the subhead, GROCER'S WIFE APPARENTLY STEPPED OFF INTO WATER WHILE IN DELIRIUM. The story talked about her headaches and poor health. I still have the clippings, which I nearly memorized when I was told about it. Two days later, the paper rehashed the whole thing in a funeral story. I remember it said, 'Friends and neighbors said she had not been in good health, which has been generally accepted as the indirect cause of the drowning. Whether or not she intentionally walked into the water or did so in a moment of delirium caused by her illness will never be known.'" Jake paused. "I guess I've gone on too long about this, Jessica, but you asked for it. My mother was always a little odd. When I found out what had happened to her mother, it helped me be more sympathetic."

Jessica hadn't moved a muscle during Jake's story. She shook her head and said, "That's unbelievably sad. All those questions and no answers. Was your grandfather guilty? Did the woman commit suicide? It must have messed up your mom. Did she get over it? Keep going, and don't skip anything. Don't worry about talking too much."

"Granddad went broke. The Pennysavers failed thanks to the combined efforts of the Depression and then the rise of supermarkets. Mom could talk about it if you pushed her. She insisted she'd gotten over it and said it didn't affect her near as much as her older sister, who was twelve when it happened. Still, I remember Mom playing the martyr for days at a time, advertising her feelings on her sleeve. I recently read an article showing that most of us have a psychological immune system, sort of, which is why we can keep going after almost anything. Look at the Holocaust survivors. But I'm not sure we're ever the same."

Jake stared into the distance for a moment. "You know, my life story's not that interesting. I don't think I can recite the whole thing without dozing off. But I got started on the family scandal, and there's no way to tell it briefly."

"You're not getting off that easily, Jake," she said, shaping her lips into a horizontal line that disclosed nothing. "You made me talk for twenty minutes straight, so you've got a long way to go."

He took a deep breath. "You ever heard of the Mountain Meadows massacre?"

"Sure," she said. "Where the Mormons murdered a whole wagon train of people coming through Utah? I've heard of it. Mountain Meadows isn't that far from here, you know. We learned about it in sixth grade."

"We associate September 11 with tragedy, after the airplane attacks," he said. "Rightly so. But there was tragedy on a September 11 long ago—1857, to be exact, in southern Utah. Luckily, they didn't murder all of them. That wagon train came from Arkansas. The Mormons didn't kill the infants. They put them in families and raised them after they killed the others. A few of those infants grew up and escaped Utah and made it back to Arkansas. One of them was my great-grandfather, the father of my grocery-store grandfather. I guess you could say

I'm lucky to be here. If the Mormons had killed baby Great-Granddad, you'd be chatting with Hee-Haw over there."

"Wow. You're living history." Jess smiled and nodded. "Did you ever know him?"

"Now I might be a year or two older than you, Miss O'Reilly, but I'm far from being that ancient. I just barely knew my grandfather. He died when I was little. The Arkansawyers migrated to Missouri by way of Oklahoma. On my dad's side of the family was his father, the one-eyed marshal of a lake town in Oklahoma. His name was Jefferson Columbus Holly. It was still pretty wild country when Dad was growing up there. There were real outlaws and semiwild Indians. I've looked up the clippings on Jefferson too. It's easy with the Internet. The best one was when he formed a horseback posse to chase a murderer on the run. It sounds like a scene from a bad movie, but the outlaw shot at the posse as they closed in, and my granddad shot back with a rifle while riding a running horse. His shot knocked the murderer down and killed him cold with one shot. Had to be a lucky shot, but Jefferson was quite the hero for a while. My dad said he was a stern, hard man. A horse had kicked out his eye when he was a teenager. He had a cheap glass eye that was cloudy. And, no, I didn't know him either." Jake paused. "You must think I come from a crazy family." He leaned back and looked at her. "Really, we're all pretty normal." He scrunched his face into a lunatic's wild-eyed scowl.

"Oh, sure, I can see that," she said with a giggle. "Now, what about school and your marriage and the rest?"

"Do I have to?"

"Yes, you have to."

Jake shrugged and held both hands open, facing up. He told her about grade school in three sentences. He described his small-town high school of three hundred students, leaving out the girlfriends and hitting the high spots of team athletics. He explained how he'd been on an athletic team of one kind or another, year round, from ages eight to eighteen. He talked about college. Despite several athletic scholarship offers, he was burned out on sports and stopped being a jock. "I went back to baseball later and played in college. After being away from athletics and teams, suddenly it was fun again. You can learn a lot in sports. College baseball is high-level competition, and I think it was good for me. A couple of big-league scouts talked to me and suggested I try pro ball, but it seemed like a dead end unless you made it big in the major leagues. The odds of that weren't good."

Taking a sip of lukewarm coffee, he continued, "Allie and I married right after college. We'd been inseparable since our senior year in high school. My degree was in hotel and restaurant management; hers was in business. Believe it or not, we both got jobs related to our degrees. It would be a better story if she worked in a hotel and I went into business—but I started with Ritz-Carlton, and she worked for a corporation that made chemicals. We wondered later on if that had anything to do with her cancer. We lived in St. Louis and loved it. But the traveling for me was brutal. That's what led us into our start-up restaurant. Looking back now, I can say we were young and enthusiastic and naïve. The first year was really hard, and we nearly failed. By working eighteen hours a day, we hung on. Everybody has a great idea for a restaurant; reality is different. Most fail in the first two years.

We liked eating healthy and thought it was time for organic, healthy food. We nearly starved at first because people talk about eating right, but they want a dripping cheeseburger when they're hungry. Allie and I called it *caveman syndrome*. Anyway, we survived, and then we finally did two things that turned it around. We changed the menu, still going for lighter foods with a nod toward eating healthy, but with recognizable items like salads, roasted chicken, well-made sandwiches on good local baguettes, tortilla wraps with chunks of grilled fish, interesting soups, that kind of thing. I remember one soup we invented called mushroom and black olive. Strange, huh? We'd give out little tasting cups, and everyone loved it. When we'd come up with something new that people liked, it was a lot of fun. The biggest change we made was adding a drive-through window. Fast-food restaurants had them, but It was a new thing for a good restaurant. Customers loved that. They could be in and out in a hurry, take things home for lunch or dinner, and it was still light eating and good food. So Live Right Express, as we called it, became a big hit, and before long we had four of them going. It was a busy time, a fun time. One day Allie came home from the doctor's office and asked me to sit down, she had something to tell me. I knew she'd been feeling run down, but we both thought it was due to hard work and long hours. When she asked me to sit down, my knees went to jelly. My hands were trembling. I couldn't breathe. Somehow, I knew. 'I've got cancer,' she said. 'It's serious. It explains why I haven't gotten pregnant.'"

Jake stared at his shoes and swallowed twice to make the lump in his throat go away. Tears formed in Jessica's eyes along with a stir in her heart that would become familiar.

"She was dead in four months. We tried everything to save her, but nothing helped. The radiation made her weak, and the chemo made her sick. The last weeks were absolute and unequivocal hell. At that point we both wished she'd skipped all the medical intervention. At least she would have felt OK for a while." Jake paused again, unable to continue, and looked up at Jessica. "I'm sorry to subject you to this."

"No, no," Jess said. "Please don't apologize. I'm really glad you told me. I can't imagine how horrible that must have been. I'm sorry that happened to you—and to her." She reached across the table and put her hand on Jake's and squeezed. It was the first time they touched. Both were aware of that milestone. They looked at each other and Jake put his hand over Jessica's and squeezed back. "Thank you for saying that. It helps. It really does. The story ends with the sale of the restaurants and moving here. Our managers covered well when Allie was sick. I was with her nearly every minute. I sold to a guy in St. Louis who already had three white-tablecloth places. The managers got promotions, and they still keep in touch with me. They've opened four more stores, two in Kansas City and two in Chicago, with more on the way."

"But maybe it's only the middle . . . or the beginning."

"What do you mean?"

"You said, 'The story ends.' It looks to me like you're well on your way to a new beginning, or at least a new middle. I hear you've got that farm standing tall and producing."

"I hope you're right. I'm ready for a new beginning."

17

CHARGES FILED AT THE COURTHOUSE

"Jessica, can I please talk to you for a minute?" Tal O'Reilly motioned his daughter to his side as Eldo and Jake entered the sheriff's back door at the county courthouse. "I understand being loyal to Jake, but please, there's no reason to drag you into this. You're putting me in an impossible position. I can't file charges on my own daughter."

"Charge Jake and you charge me," Jess said. Challenge spewed from her voice and manner. "You say you're filing a murder charge against the man I love—and want to spend the rest of my life with—because you have to. You say you're doing the job you were elected to do. You know perfectly well that if Jake is a criminal then I'm an accessory. So do your job. Send us both to prison."

Tal leaned against the doorframe. His breathing was troubled, his complexion ruddy. His head shook from side to side. "You just said you love him. You've never told me that. Are you going to marry him?"

"Dad, I would marry him in a New York second if he asked. I'm hoping he'll have me. Why would I tell you I love him? You still think I'm about fourteen, but I've been a grown woman for quite a while. A grown woman doesn't discuss her love life with her father. I know you think he's too old for me, but, Dad, Jake isn't that crudbag Louise married. Furthest thing from it. You're blind to him because he's older or maybe you'd see what I'm saying. This isn't the time or place to discuss it— but, yes, I love him. And, yes, I hope to marry him."

"OK," Tal said softly. "OK. Maybe you're right. Maybe I don't know him that well. Will you help me understand?"

"As long as you have an open mind."

"I still have to bring charges against him. What else can I do? Who knows what DNA circulates in that creature he killed? You realize Aurora is going to be overrun with media and every Bigfoot nut in the country. I'm guessing there'll be some government folks come visiting too. What a mess."

"You're probably right."

"So would you please not insist on being an accessory?"

"Sorry, I insist. Either do your job gung-ho or figure out something else."

Tal took a deep breath and exhaled through his nose. His complexion turned from ruddy to wan. It went against every instinct to involve his daughter in the jumble before him. He was cornered, exactly like the time Jessica was in seventh grade and had asserted herself by insisting she was old enough to go to movies with friends, no parents allowed. Tal had wanted to protect her from pedophiles and kidnappers by saying no, but he knew he would alienate her. He relented— and worried every minute she was out of his sight.

He knew he could drop the charges later at his discretion. He said, "OK." He gave her a look so she knew he was stricken. "Let's fill out the forms and have Eldo take you back."

Twenty minutes later, Eldo dropped Jess and Jake at the rear door of the Marsh Funeral Home. Oscar was long gone. Eldo piped up with what, for him, was a speech. "I hope both of you know I don't agree with what he's doing. He's worried about what people will think. We're in for a helluva week. I've got twenty phone messages, and that's the tip of the iceberg. Tal asked me to say nothing except that there will be a public statement later on, so I'll have Tina in my office start calling them back. He wants to meet Oscar here to make a video."

"Thanks, Eldo," Jake said. "We understand you're doing your job. It'll all come out in the wash. Hey, thanks for the ride."

As Eldo drove away, Jake turned to Jess. He tried to be relaxed and upbeat. Athletics taught him well—the tighter the squeeze, the looser you need to be.

"What's with the furrowed brow?" he asked. "Pretend we're in Hawaii. Hang loose." He made the island signal with thumb and pinkie. He poked her in the ribs with his index finger. "Jessie, Jessie, Jessie," he teased.

She relaxed and smiled.

"Come on, little darlin'. Let's go jogging. I need exercise. You may be still in diapers, but this old jock might wear you out. If you'll go jogging with me, I'll make lunch. Let's get cookies for dessert."

"You're on," she said.

They drove toward the local bakery and hot dog joint, a former bank building naturally called First National Frank and Crust. Jess put her hand on Jake's arm and said, "I can't begin to tell you how sorry I am this is happening, Jacob. I feel like it's my fault because he's my father. You must be worried. What can I do?"

"Worried? Sure. Well, not really. OK, maybe a little. Who knows where this is headed? I just hope we don't end up on Court TV. He's right, though—a big fuss is on the way. It would be more interesting if we weren't in the middle of it. Jess, let me say this once more: I wish you hadn't insisted that he bring you into it. When I tried to talk you out of it on the way to the courthouse, I was as serious as a heart attack. You wouldn't listen to me or to him. I understand what you're doing. I love you for it. But I wish you hadn't put yourself in the middle."

"Why, thank you, Mr. Holly. I love you too. By the way, you may not have noticed, but I doubt he could convict either of us for anything."

"Why is that?"

"Because Eldo didn't get back to reading us our rights. He skipped the Miranda warning. He started with you and then stopped. I've got a sneaky feeling the big ape did it on purpose."

18

FUNERAL HOME 3—VIDEO THE BEAST

Oscar unlocked the cold room and checked the thermostat. Thirty-three degrees on the button. He pulled back the rubberized sheet and watched with Eldo as O'Reilly prepared to videotape the Sasquatch corpse with an outdated Sony camcorder. "Good Lord, will you look at this thing?" Tal muttered. "He said he brought her to town on an Indian sled. That's impressive."

"I'll stay out of it, if you don't mind," Oscar said. "You know, Tal, actually, you should charge me too, don't you think? I helped them. Jess was more loyal to Jake than I was, but the more I think about it—"

"Now, Oscar, don't you start on me. This hasn't been a good day so far, to say the least. Let's get this video made and move along. We've been telling folks I'd make an announcement of some kind today. I need to figure out what to say."

Tal turned his attention back to the remains. "Look at that hair and those fingernails. They're not clean by our standards, but for an animal? Look at the feet. My God. The name fits, doesn't it? I wonder how many of these things are out there. I wonder if she had any little ones."

"What do you want us to do?" Eldo asked.

"The best thing would be to pop your eyeballs back in and keep watch on the door," Tal said. "We definitely don't want anyone walking in."

"Can do."

"OK, Oscar, if you would, take this tape measure I brought, and I'll aim the camera and do the talking while you stretch the tape. I'll call out what we're measuring. Is that a plan?"

Oscar looked Tal in the eye, telegraphing his disappointment about the situation with Jake and Jess. "Sure," he said coolly.

Tal turned on the camcorder and swung it around to the corpse. The camera's light was strong. It cast sinister shadows on the cold room wall that made the video look like a scene from *The Blair Witch Project*. He aimed his head at the built-in microphone and spoke in a speechmaker's voice:

"For the record, this is Talburt O'Reilly, prosecuting attorney for Cispus County, Washington. We're videotaping the body of an unidentified creature lying in the Marsh Funeral Home in Aurora, Washington. With me is Oscar Marsh, the funeral director. Sheriff Eldo Throckmorton is nearby. We're making a tape to form a reference document for this creature. I have looked on the Internet and found protocols regarding standards of measurement and description for primate limbs in dead specimens, but we aren't scientists. Therefore, we won't be using biological or medical terms. Since our instrument is a simple tape measure, all numbers should be considered approximate.

"As you can see, Oscar is measuring the total length of this female creature at about seven feet, eight inches, or a total of ninety-two inches and probably a bit more. He is extending the leg as best he can, but the subject is way too long for the gurney. Now we're measuring her arm length. Over forty-seven inches from shoulder blade to fingertip, and we're getting ninety-six inches all the way across her back from fingertip to fingertip. Those are long arms.

"Oscar, let's measure her head, please, from the chin to the top." Tal zoomed the camera for a close look at the Sasquatch's face and head, as well as the tape. "A little more than seventeen inches. Oscar, hold the tape on your own head that same way. As you can see, Oscar's head is less than ten inches vertically. OK, now the feet." The tape was stretched heel to toe on the creature's left foot. Both men looked carefully at the result, and Tal held the camera steadily on the tape. "Twenty-seven inches or more," he said. "Good Lord."

Tal reversed the zoom and pulled back for a wider view as he continued the narration and Oscar moved the tape from place to place. "I would describe the hair color as reddish brown," Tal said, "and the subject is very hairy below the shoulders, less so above. Her head hair seems intentionally arranged. As you can see in the face structure and proportion, whatever this creature is, she has a lot in common with us. The bullet wound I'm focusing on now was made by a large-caliber rifle fired at relatively close range. The man who fired the shot was detained and charged with a crime, then released on his own recognizance. He is known in our community and says the shooting was accidental; also, he says there was a male creature present who was slightly wounded in the shoulder when the shot was fired. As previously stated, we've made this video account to document the existence of the creature and to help us sort out what to do next. There are many rumors in our area and elsewhere about this event. We intend to make a public announcement later today. This concludes our recording."

Tal removed the videocassette from the camera as Oscar replaced the rubber sheet over the Sasquatch. Tal knitted his eyebrows at Oscar and asked, "Where should we put this tape?"

"Leave it right here, I guess," Oscar said. "You and I have the only keys to the lock on this room."

"Perfect." Tal tucked the tape next to the body on the covered gurney. They locked up, gathered Eldo, and departed.

19

POTUS BREAKS THE REVERIE

The O'Reilly house in Aurora was locally famous and often referred to by the nickname Ol' Vic. It was a sterling example of Victorian architecture from the Belle Époque, built by a late-nineteenth-century lumber baron with a crew of local craftsmen and Chinese laborers. Jessica was born and raised in the house along with an older brother and sister who moved away to become computer geeks in Seattle. The outside was a blizzard of gingerbread, shingles, and porches. The inside featured plaster curlicues, a room for every purpose, and a few rooms without a clear purpose. There were hideouts under stairways and behind closets where kids could secret themselves with friends.

Jessica's house was where all the girls, and sometimes the boys, wanted to hang out after school. She loved the house, just as she loved the way her mother, Ruth, had furnished it. Everything was traditional. Large antiques stood sentry duty; nothing was changed. Many of the dark, wood furnishings hadn't moved in more than three decades, not since Tal and Ruth and their oldest son moved in. Ol' Vic could have served as a museum for admirers of Queen Victoria and Prince Albert. At the bottom of the main staircase, two ornate newel-posts anchored a curvy handrailing and balusters leading up. The O'Reilly children had designated one of the posts the Honor Post, declaring that when anyone was touching it, they must not under any circumstances tell a lie. Only the absolute truth was acceptable. Not even an exaggeration was allowed. To anyone's knowledge, the vow was never violated. The system quickly became useful to the children as a way to hold each other's claims to the fire. Later, they let their parents in on the pledge. Eventually, the obligation was modified so that simply by stating "Honor Post" at the end of a story, the truth of the matter was established. No one broke the Honor Post. All were equally honor bound.

Tal O'Reilly was thinking about the Honor Post as he sat in his study off the main parlor. The room was called a sewing room when the house was built, despite its masculine patterned-tin ceiling and burled mahogany paneling. Tal's arm dangled off a leather wing chair, his hand twisting his tortoise-shell reading glasses. He remembered the day just after her sixth birthday when Jessica denied leaving jelly mushed into the peanut butter and forgetting the lid. "Jess, come here for a second." His words were twenty years gone, but came back like it happened yesterday. "Now, honey," he said, with kindness in his tone, "put your hand on the Honor Post. OK. Now, did you get the jelly in the peanut butter and leave the lid off?"

"Daddy, that's not fair. Do I have to answer?"

Tal remembered laughing. "No, honey pie. I think you've already answered, haven't you?"

"It was an accident. I just forgot. I'm sorry."

"Thank you for telling the truth, my little beauty. You know, I think I'll always keep you at six years old. You're a perfect daughter right now."

"Thank you, Daddy. Can I go now?"

"Have fun. See you later."

"Bye." And away she ran.

Parents know, and fear, that one day their children will disappoint them. They try not to believe it, especially when the kids are small. Later, their concern is often justified. Tal had always known the axiom but put no faith in it, at least when it came to his youngest. Jessica's life was a seemingly endless string of successes. Her father was always proud of her, and never more than when she chose law as a career and was good at it.

Then came the romance with an older man—Jake. Tal was blindsided. It agitated him like he'd eaten something disagreeable. At sixty-one, Tal had developed a bum knee and the fragile digestion that comes with age. An enviable adulthood of rich dinners and desserts had caused his chest to slip to his beltline, and it took a while to get out of bed. His reverie about the Honor Post made him smile. His glasses slid to the floor, jerking his thoughts back to the present. He picked up the glasses and put them on while fetching a piece of lined paper. He began to write in longhand the announcement he intended to make to the citizens of Aurora, and thereby the world, in about an hour. Eldo had spread the word at Hee-Haw's and elsewhere that anyone interested should be on the courthouse lawn at one o'clock.

Tal threw away his first effort and started on a fresh sheet. He wrote carefully, in a deliberately small and surprisingly artistic hand with a fine-point Mont Blanc pen. It was Tal's habit when he needed to speak in public to write out in longhand what he wanted to say. Doing so gave him total recall as he spoke. Rarely did he need to glance at what he'd written.

Thanks to all of you for coming on short notice. You've probably heard the rumors flying around town. That's what we're here to talk about. We live in a part of the world that's very familiar with what is usually called Bigfoot. There's not a person here who hasn't been in a discussion or an argument over Bigfoot. We've all heard the stories. But we'd all like to know: Is there such a thing or not?

My friends and neighbors, we don't have to wonder any longer. Now we know. You've heard the buzz, and as your elected official, I've been involved in getting to the bottom of it. Yesterday afternoon, our own Jake Holly was riding his gelding in the national forest a few miles from where we're standing when he shot and killed a female Bigfoot—Sasquatch, if you prefer. He somehow rigged up an Indian sled and brought the body to town. It's under lock and key right here, right now. Most of you know my daughter Jessica. She drove out to meet Jake and helped him bring it in.

When the outside world gets wind of this, as you can imagine, Aurora will be the center of the universe for a while. To tell you the truth, I was a skeptic about Bigfoot. But I've seen this creature lying dead, so I'm not a skeptic anymore. She looks a lot more human than the drawings and carvings you've seen. Jake reports that there was a male with her. He says the shooting was an accident. Some people have insisted if anyone ever found a Bigfoot and shot it, it would be a crime. Other folks thought we should shoot it so scientists could learn about a previously unknown species. So I had a decision to make. . . .

It took a third ring of the phone to break Tal's concentration.

"Ruthie, can you get that?" he yelled. But Ruth was in the potting shed. It was time to plant flowers. Tal put paper and pen aside and crossed the room to his desk phone. He picked it up on the fifth ring and looked out the bay window. The steam cloud above St. Helens was higher and wider than any time since she awoke a few days ago.

"Hello, this is Tal O'Reilly."

"Good day, Mr. O'Reilly. The sheriff's office told us we could catch up with you at this number. My name is Stanton Buckley. I'm calling from the White House in Washington, DC." Tal looked away from the mountain and unconsciously squared his shoulders. He was about to speak, but Buckley continued. "I'm the chief of staff for the president, sir, and we're calling you on a matter of considerable importance."

"Yes, Mr. Buckley. I guess I should assume this isn't a joke."

"Mr. O'Reilly, the president would like to speak to you. This isn't a prank. I imagine you'll have no trouble recognizing his voice. Would that be OK with you?"

"Yes. Of course."

"Then I'll put him on. This is a secure line, Mr. O'Reilly. May I say in advance as I hand him the phone that we deeply appreciate your cooperation."

"Good afternoon, Mr. O'Reilly." The familiar voice was crystal clear and full of charm. "Or is it still morning there? I've got almost exactly three o'clock here, so that would make it noon there, right?"

"Good afternoon, Mr. President. Yes, sir, exactly noon. I'm honored by your call. Thank you for all you do."

"Well, I sure appreciate that. Believe me, a kind word in Washington is hard to come by. May I call you Tal?"

"Of course."

"Tal, I'm told we may have a delicate situation there in your community. If you don't mind, I'd like to discuss it with you."

20

JOURNALISTS' CHANCE MEETING

Although it was unlikely to the extreme, a journalist from India and another from Japan met in a bar in the main terminal of Tokyo's Narita International Airport and discovered they were chasing the same story. When Ashok Mahadevan ordered apple juice and paid with his credit card, the bartender asked for additional identification. Not wanting to dig for his passport, Ashok laid out his picture card with journalistic credentials, and it caught the eye of Kenzo Matsuki, who was nursing a glass of American bourbon nearby. When Ashok moved to a small table to await his flight to San Francisco, Kenzo decided to introduce himself to his fellow scribe.

After exchanging pleasantries in accented English and beginning a conversation, the two were soon shaking their heads and slapping the table at the irony of both of them chasing the Internet Sasquatch story to Washington State in the United States.

"Why go New Delhi to here Tokyo?" Kenzo asked. "Not better go west to London from India?"

119

"Actually it's about the same either direction," Ashok said. "It depends largely on the connections." His accent was a lovely mixture of Hindi and colonial English. "The next plane toward Europe was several hours away, but if I hurried, I could get to Tokyo and have a short wait to San Francisco. I can't believe we are both on the same quest. I'm not sure I believe any of it, do you?"

"I believe. My boss no believe. He say, 'Kenzo, you find good story, *Morning Star* pay expense. You no find, you pay.' I tell him, 'Bye-bye.'"

Kenzo and Ashok were so different from each other an alien zoologist might have taken them for separate species. Their visual aspects set them apart, to be sure, but it was their diets that made them cosmic opposites.

Ashok, whose name meant "without sorrow," had been vegetarian since birth. Never once had he consumed fish or fowl or meat. His Brahman mother had raised him on milk and honey, fruit, and vegetables spiced a thousand ways, all of them succulent. As an adult he had a continuing curiosity about other ways of eating, including meat, but not yet enough to drive him to sample. His health was superb; he was thin and vigorous with skin the color of latte. Ashok wore John Lennon glasses that gave him an owlish visage, white shirts with the sleeves rolled up, and narrow ties a decade out of style. He chose his words carefully and spoke softly, which usually commanded attention.

Kenzo, on the other hand, was bullheaded to a point just shy of cocky. His name meant "wise" or sometimes "three." He got to the point quickly and with noticeable volume. He was an unrepentant omnivore and proud of it. Sometimes he'd declare the only thing he wouldn't eat was something he couldn't reach; at other times, he'd assert the only thing he wouldn't eat was something that ate him first. The plate of airport sashimi he was washing down with his bourbon was clear evidence of his appetites. Though only thirty-three, Kenzo showed evidence of a well-earned and mounting avoirdupois. He joked that his next career would be in sumo. He was an excellent reporter but a star trencherman—having consumed, he told Ashok, goat, crocodile, wagyu beef, puffer fish, whale, live octopus, squid by the bushel, shark's fin, bird's nest, snake, fermented eggs, buffalo, elk, bear, dog, horse, and an impressive array of exotic fowl. His raven-black hair was buzzed into a longish flattop. His English was so basic it deserved the description *broken*, but his opinions rendered in any language were firmly held. He made Ashok mildly nauseated as he tossed down raw pieces of fish like popcorn and chased them with Kentucky firewater.

"We get Toyota San Francisco," Kenzo said. "Go Washington together. Long time drive. You drive too, yes?"

"Sorry. I've never really driven much. Never had a reason."

"No problem. I teach."

"You said we would drive a long time. Isn't Washington fairly close to San Francisco? How long do we drive to get there?"

"Many hours. America big."

"Yes, of course it is," Ashok said. "But on a map Washington and San Francisco are not that far apart."

"Not drive on map. Drive on road."

"I was planning to take a bus or train. But we'll do whatever it takes to get to Aurora, Washington, no doubt. Hey, they're calling our flight. Let's go."

21

JAKE'S—BURN THE BLOOD AND HAIR

Jessie and Jake finished their jog and returned to Jake's for lunch. Despite his earlier promise, Jess insisted she wanted to cook the mound of baby vegetables he'd set aside, so Jake went to the barn to care for Split Log. He saw the limbs from the travois alongside the tent canvas lying next to the horse's stall where he'd left them the night before. A closer look revealed dabs of dried blood and hair on the rigging, ropes, and canvas. He finished his horse chores—feeding, watering, brushing—then picked up the travois material and leaned it against the barn wall. His face was expressionless, his movements determined. Jake took his hatchet from the saddlebag and began to hack the sled into small pieces. His blows were swift and accurate and forceful. He made a bundle of it all and headed toward the house.

Jake moved to the rear patio, where he'd installed a brick fire pit and a wood bin. Sizzling meat and a warm fire with wine in hand fueled many pleasant hours of conversation between Jess and Jake. He didn't pause as he dumped the canvas, ropes, and tree limbs into the fire pit as if they offended him. From the storage box came dry matches, kindling, and logs. Within a minute, the bundle was ablaze. Jake gave the flame a stir and watched silently, peering into the burning mess as if hypnotized. Several minutes passed. He turned away and entered the kitchen through the back door. Jessica watched him through the window.

"Hey, madam chef," Jake said as he entered. "Smells good in here. I see you're grilling them on the Jenn-Air. Did you find the good olive oil in the pantry?"

"I did indeed. The hardest thing to find was a brush. By now you'd think I'd know where you keep things. I also brushed olive oil on the baguette and rubbed it with one of your fresh garlic bulbs. That's on the grill, and maybe that's what you smell. Speaking of which, I need to get the baguette off." She tonged the split French loaf off the hot grill. "You looked busy out there. Would you care to discuss your pyromaniac urge?"

He picked up the used violin he'd bought on eBay and stared at the sheet music from his last lesson. He played a half dozen scale notes, each of them clear and competent. "I've been trying to explain it to myself. The travois I used to carry her was in the barn. When I finished with Splitty, something possessed me to tear it apart and burn it. You could still see a little blood and hair. I don't know, I guess I got to thinking about your dad and Eldo and God knows who else rummaging through my barn. It seemed wise to get rid of it. I'm feeling nervous about all this. I've lost control of my life."

"It's happening so fast," Jess said. "When do we sit down and catch our breath and think it all through? For example, are we going to Dad's meeting at the courthouse after lunch, or are you going to play me a concert, Paganini?"

"I don't see the point of going. We know what he'll say. They've already gone to Swampy's and made a video. He's going to tell the world. *Mucho malo problemo.* I'd rather stay here and not answer the phone."

"That's what I thought you'd say." Jess plucked vegetables off the grill. Crisscross grill marks scarred the little carrots, red and yellow heirloom tomatoes, Brussels sprouts, fingerling potatoes, and green beans. "Hey, this is ready. You up for a glass of that pinot gris with lunch?"

"Sounds perfect. Let me flare up my fire again. Back in a sec." Jake hustled to the fire and stirred the contents. He thought of squeezing in a stream of starter fluid, but anything not already ash blazed up again on its own. He looked into the distance and saw that the cloud of gas and steam from St. Helens was larger than yesterday. It moved upward with greater imperative than when he'd watched it through the giant trees and been amazed.

22

BIG LIE AT THE COURTHOUSE

Tal O'Reilly held up his paws like Elmer Gantry about to unleash fire and brimstone. His dark suit and white shirt commanded the respect of a vestment. He had a sturdy physique that brought to mind a lapsed weightlifter, and his shrewd features wore a bemused expression. The bright morning sun had yielded to El Niño, ushering in a gray and sprinkly afternoon. Hee-Haw's was as empty as if the Rapture had begun. Aurorians scattered across the courthouse lawn were chattering and gesturing with each other, drawn by the Bigfoot rumor like moths to flame. The small-town grapevine had operated at maximum efficiency. Everyone wanted to know about the Sasquatch.

"Good afternoon, everyone. May I have your attention, please?" Tal turned up his unamplified volume to short-circuit the buzz and smiled at his fellow citizens as if bestowing a benediction. "*Hello?* Thank you for coming out on short notice. It looks like Eldo did a good job of getting the word out."

"Hey, Tal! Where's the monster? My boy seen it." The voice belonged to Edgar Lasswell, who obviously had a head start from Hee-Haw's keg tap.

"Now hold on a minute, Ed," Tal said. "Just hold up with that. I've heard the scuttlebutt just like you have, that somebody came dragging a Sasquatch into town last night. We'll get to that in a minute. I'm here to talk about the mountain. Surely all of you have noticed the smoke and steam are bigger and higher today. She's wide awake. We need to know what's going on."

Disappointment vibrated through the crowd. Tal paused and cleared his throat. He looked seriously at his neighbors while knitting his brow and pursing his lips. Lasswell piped up again before Tal could continue. "What're you saying, Tal? You know everybody watches the mountain reports on TV. They're saying it's no big deal. We thought you come to tell us about the Bigfoot. Now, what's the deal on that?"

Tal feigned amazement and looked from face to face. "Is Ed right about that?" he said to no one in particular. "Did you folks come here thinking I was going to talk about another Bigfoot rumor? Don't we get enough of those around here? Sure, I've heard it, and Eldo and I have checked into it as best we can at this point. I can't say if there's anything to it or not. If it's like most of them, it'll turn out somebody was poaching a deer or hauling off a dead cow." Tal was careful about what he said. He didn't lie openly because as a good politician, he knew it might come back to haunt him.

"Now," he continued, "if this is a downer, I'm sorry. It's looking like more rain, so let me get on with it. As soon as I'm able to tell you anything for sure about the rumor, I'll spread the word. I'll even stop in at Hee-Haw's and buy a round. But for the moment, we need to keep one eye on the mountain. I talked with the boys from USGS up there watching her not a half hour ago. They're still not worried about a big eruption like 1980, but she may go on grumbling for quite a while. They're predicting a wind shift this afternoon, along with an inversion layer, which means we may get dusted with smoke and ash right here in Aurora. I don't believe I'll be washing my car this weekend." Tal looked around for comic effect but saw only a few weak smiles. "Folks can get a little panicky when ash starts blowing around, so please pass the word. The mountain guys say not to worry. We should try to stay inside. If it gets thick and you have to be outside, breathe through a handkerchief. Thank you for coming out, and a good day to everyone."

Tal stepped down from the courthouse steps and gave Eldo and Oscar the let's-go signal. The townspeople watched him walk away. A few lowered their chins and shook their heads in disapproval. Others looked confused. Necks craned and eyebrows arched while mutters of disfavor rustled through the group. They wanted a Sasquatch. They got a letdown.

Eldo and Oscar looked at Tal expectantly as the three escaped to their vehicles. From the side of his mouth, Tal quietly said, "Meet me in five minutes at the Ultra Mart parking lot. I need to tell you about a phone call."

23

HEE-HAW'S 2—THE MISFITS GATHER

"There's something he's not telling us. No way he'd make a big deal out of a little ash from Helens. Hell, with all the rain, nobody's gonna wash a car." The speaker was Albert Swearingen, Hee-Haw himself, and his Saturday regulars nodded in agreement. "I don't know what's going on, but we need to figure how to smoke old Tal out. Get him tell us what he knows. Eldo will never say a word, you can bet on that."

"Hey," Edgar Lasswell interrupted. "Did you notice that Swampy Marsh walked off with him and Eldo? My boy says the Bigfoot that grabbed him was down there behind Oscar's funeral home, and he saw Oscar and those other people wheeling something into the building. What do you think?"

There was silence as the information was digested. The one called LR said, "He could be in on it. If your boy's story is even half-true—and if somebody brung a dead Bigfoot to town—where would they put it? The funeral home would be a darn good place. Maybe we orta go down there and take a look."

"Swampy would have it locked up tighter'n a tick's ass," Hee-Haw said. "I don't allow we want to go breaking into a funeral home this time of day."

"Then, by God, let's go down there as soon as it starts getting dark," Lasswell said. "My boy don't lie, and I want to know what's going on."

LR stared at Lasswell. Most Aurorians had gone home frustrated but defeated by the prosecuting attorney's diversion at the courthouse. Hee-Haw's hard-core regulars, however, had reassembled and were in full constabulary mode. They awaited the next pronouncement like military recruits. "Any of you ever spend time out in the woods?" LR asked the group. "If you did, you couldn't have any doubt there might be a great big ol' thing wandering around. It's like a jungle, only the trees and bushes and bugs are on steroids. Frogs the size of footballs. Spiders you could throw a saddle on and ride. Flowers big as pie plates. You get out there five miles and you might as well be five thousand miles away. If somebody found us a Bigfoot, I won't be surprised. I always told you they was out there. Hell, we'll rename this place Monster, Washington. Everybody'll wanna come see it—and we won't be talking about some chawbacon out there with fake feet. We'll have the real thing." LR grinned and displayed his tea-colored, tree-stump teeth. "My little old motel will get a hundred a night and be full year-round. I'll finally be a rich man."

Hee-Haw shook his head. "We'd be glad if you were rich, LR. Maybe you'd buy us a round once in a while. And maybe you'd get a better car to park by my front door. Hey,

why don't you get one with fenders made out of diamonds?
You keep getting drunk and scraping things. Your old jalopy's
got more lumps than a sack of doorknobs."

24

ULTRA MART—THE SECRET IS OUT

The sheriff's Crown Vic, a Jeep, and a Tahoe pulled into the Ultra Mart parking lot within a minute of each other. All drove to the rear, near the Dumpster. Eldo got out and leaned on the squad car. Tal and Oscar parked and joined him, forming a loose circle. The men looked at Tal expectantly.

"This one's hard to believe," Tal began.

Eldo and Oscar slanted disbelieving looks at Tal.

"Before I get started, let me assure you gentlemen this is the truth. I'm not kidding, or, as my kids used to say, this is on the Honor Post. A little while ago, I got a phone call from the president of the United States. How the devil they knew about this so fast, I have no earthly idea. But for sure they know something has happened and they asked us to zip it up for now. He asked me how many people know, and I told him just five—Jake and Jess and us three. He's got his people on the way. They should be here later this evening or in the morning."

Tal detailed the rest of his conversation with the president.

Eldo recalled that his office clerk mentioned someone had gotten Tal's home number by convincing her it was an emergency.

Tal told his conspirators that the executive branch apparently has an elite squad of about fifty people trained and on call to deal with unusual situations, particularly if the president thought national security was involved. "They're called the PNG, the acronym for Paranormal Group," Tal said, explaining that they were on standby alert for anything unusual that called for discreet handling. They were part of the National Security Agency. "He said they were getting lots of 'blowback,' that's what he called it, about someone shooting a Sasquatch. He's worried about a public stampede and a media circus here. I told him everything, including about the video. He wanted to know where it was and was pleased that we have it under lock and key."

The trio stood behind the convenience store, out of sight, and discussed the situation for five minutes. Tal asked Eldo to use his cell phone to call Jake and Jessica to request their silence. Eldo tried them both. "No answer at either place," he reported.

Tal said, "They're probably together and out hiking or something. I'll try them as soon as I get home, or I'll drive out there and find them." The men prepared to adjourn to their homes. "I'll call you as soon as I hear from the federal guys," Tal said in parting. "The president said the PNG would call me as soon as they have boots on the ground."

25

OL' VIC—LITTLE SISTER SPEAKS HER MIND

Tal's sister Louise was in Ol' Vic's potting shed with his wife, Ruthie, handing her a bag of soil for gardenias. A grow light shone directly overhead and unflatteringly on Louise's plain features and on her backside, which had grown wider than an ax handle. Tal walked into Ol' Vic and heard voices in the back, so he joined the women. Louise was fifty-six years old, five years younger than Tal. She'd been protected and coddled by her big brother from the day she was born. Right now she didn't look happy.

"Hello, Talby. I was hoping you'd come along," she said as she washed her hands in the mop sink. "Ruth thought you'd be back. I need to chat with you."

Tal noted the tincture of knowingness in his sister's eyes and realized the chat would not be about the weather. "Let's go to my office," he said. "You want some coffee? Or a Coke?"

"Haven't you got any fancy wine open?" she asked. "It's Saturday. Let's have a glass. Hell's bells, it's way past happy hour in London." She smirked at the ancient joke.

"You're right, little sister. The limeys are pouring Pimm's cup. I just happen to have a dry Riesling ready to go and it is good, good, good." He detoured through the kitchen and brought the bottle and two glasses. "We opened this last night, but I had to leave for a while and we didn't get back to it. This wine got big ratings and was compared to the best from Alsace-Lorraine. It was actually made not far from here."

"All I know is, every time you pour me a glass of wine, I like it," Louise said. "Make mine a big glass. I don't care if it's from hereabouts or someplace that sounds like the old actress Laraine Day or squeezed out of Hee-Haw's bar towels. I know if you're pouring it, it'll go down fine. Now sit down and lean back while I let you in on something."

Louise and Tal sipped the Riesling appreciatively. Tal swirled his glass and checked the color and viscosity of the wine, then began a soliloquy praising the particular virtues of this grape. He noted that Riesling had been the king of grapes and the choice of European royalty until the twentieth century, when its lofty standing was eroded by drier white wines from Chardonnay grapes.

Louise sipped for a moment and listened. She knew more about wine—and life in general—than she let on.

"Now, Talby," she began softly, using her nickname for him from the time she could talk. "I hear about something that troubles me." Louise was capable, when agitated, of bellowing like a sauropod across the Mesozoic swamp. But she was more compelling, if not downright malevolent, when she lowered the volume and looked her prey in the eye. Tal had experienced the mood before. He was the snail and she had the saltshaker.

"Do you want descendants?" she asked.

"What? What do you mean?"

"You heard me. You know what I mean. Do you want descendants? Do you want your children to have their own children? Do you want grandchildren to keep you company in your old age?"

"Of course I do. Who wouldn't? Why are you asking?"

"Because from what I hear, you're screwing up your best chance. Your kids Ewing and Deb who moved away are fine people. But both of them are totally involved in big-city life and computers and whatnot. They may have kids someday. They may not. In Jessica you have a great daughter and a wonderful person who stayed close to home. Now you're interfering in her love life. Talby, I can figure these things out. She would never talk about such a thing to me, but I'm pretty good at reading between the lines. Jess loves you. She respects you. But you don't approve of Jake. 'Don't approve' may be putting it mildly, but I'm just guessing.

"Well, here's the thing. I'm trying to figure out what you don't like about him. I've met him and talked to him. They even took me out to dinner. Then I put two and two together. The only thing makes you hesitate is that he's—what?—fourteen or fifteen years older than Jess. I try to figure why that would be such a big deal to you. Then, bingo, it comes to me. It's Clyde. Clyde was older than I was, and the drunken, mealymouthed weasel turned out to be stupid, abusive, and a liar to boot.

"Talby, if I'm wrong about this, if you know something I don't, now would be the time to tell me. It pains me terribly to think you might be getting in the way of her happiness because of something that happened to me. To *me*. Get it? Not you or anyone else. I married Clyde because I hoped I could change him. I couldn't. He wasn't any different before or after. It was my mistake and mine alone. I know now that you can't change someone into what you think they ought to be. It was a tragedy of my own making. I'm well aware I'm not the loveliest orchid in the rain forest. I thought Clyde was my best shot at *Ozzie and Harriet* and the white picket fence. My bad, as the kids say. Nothing to do with your daughter and her man. I think you need to hear that directly from me, so there it is.

"You're well read when it comes to law, but this is philosophy. Aristotle, I believe, taught that our tragedies come from our strengths, not our weaknesses. My trauma with Clyde was a result of my virtues, not my defects. I've made peace with that. I'm asking you to listen to your little sister now. Make nice with Jake. Jessica has to figure out if he's the one. There's no other way. Never has been, never will be. Step back, Talby, and let nature take its course. It's going to whether you like it or not. There. I've had my say."

Tal had watched and listened to his sister with intensity. She was seldom so eloquent. He arose and crossed the room to the bookshelves, running his finger along the title spines. Somewhere, he knew there was an Aristotle. The room was quiet. He lifted a dusty, long unseen volume and turned smiling to his sister. He showed her the title and moved closer to offer a hug.

26

HIGHWAY—OOPS, WRONG WAY

Kenzo got his Toyota. With Ashok doing the talking, the jet-lagged journalists rented a white Corolla on Kenzo's international driver's license and crept through the maze of ramps and overpasses surrounding San Francisco International Airport. They managed to mount Highway 101 despite the traffic, which was inescapable even on a Saturday. Kenzo had the hang of the car immediately. He was an excellent driver. The unlikely pair was soon cruising at freeway speed with the windows half-down, the soft California air reviving them after the long flight from Tokyo. They had arrived before they started, backtracking against the sun and across the International Date Line. When Ashok read the first of several Palo Alto exit signs and consulted his airport-bookstore map, he was reluctant to inform his partner they were going the wrong way. He was the one who had pointed to the 101 ramp that got them on the freeway. At the second sign for Palo Alto, Ashok said timidly, "Uhh, Kenzo, I'm sorry, but it seems we're going the wrong way."

"Wrong way? Why wrong way? Water on left."

"Yes, but apparently that is something called the Back Bay. We are in Palo Alto going south toward Los Angeles."

"Damn. Hell. Son beetch," Kenzo growled like a samurai, showing off his English profanity. "I turn around next exit. You say best way then."

Ashok studied his map as they turned around. He began to confidently call out navigating instructions. They crossed the Dumbarton Bridge across the Back Bay and motored through south Oakland freeways eastward through Livermore and on to Interstate 5 northbound. Sacramento and Northern California's rugged redwood forests and woodsy villages lay ahead. The scribes tried to figure out how many miles they would drive before rolling into southwest Washington. They were Don Quixotes on a quest to Aurora, jousting at Bigfoot instead of windmills. Ashok eventually calculated the distance at about five hundred fifty miles—nine or ten hours of nonstop driving.

"I warn America big place," Kenzo said. "You think we no drive far to Washington, but I now say damn hell I surprise too. That one end Japan to other. Time you learn driving. I no drive nine ten hours."

After a quiet thirty minutes of driving, Kenzo parked the Corolla at a rest stop. Both men relieved themselves in the questionable bathroom, and Ashok's first driving lesson began. He was an intelligent adult learning in a vehicle that required no clutching or shifting, so he quickly mastered steering around the rest stop and accelerating smoothly. It was the stopping that caused the problem.

"Damn, hell, pee-pee," the samurai growled when Ashok stood the car on its nose and shot him forward for the second time. "You got too strong foot. Stop easy."

"I'm really trying, Kenzo. It feels like it's not going to stop. Do you think I can drive on that big highway? Those trucks scare me even when you're driving."

"You right. I keep drive. Much awake now."

27

LOOWIT—A LADY'S FACELIFT

The lady was giving herself a facelift. After blasting away part of her circular cone in the furious explosion and eruption of 1980, Mount St. Helens was forming a proportional magma headdress to replace the blemish. Frequent El Niño rains had little effect on the superheated pumice and ash boiling up from the earth's intestines. Rain to a volcano was a fan in a hurricane. The fiery rock, which USGS infrared instruments clocked at thirteen hundred degrees, found the path of least resistance around the missing north side and built up a new cone wall. The unhurried plume of steam, smoke, and grit was visible from a hundred miles in every direction. The sparse population in nearby rural Washington, such as the people of Aurora, scanned the sky nervously between showers. Pilots reported the cloud ascending to far above fifty thousand feet and aircraft scheduled to go anywhere near the plume were grounded. USGS volcanologists insisted that a big eruption wasn't likely, despite the continuing small earthquakes and oozing molten rock. In 1980, they didn't foresee the sideways blast that caused unprecedented devastation and loss of life—so this time, just in case they were underestimating the danger, the areas immediately around Loowit were evacuated. But the mountain seemed more concerned about reshaping herself.

When the first *Homo sapiens* rovers crossed the Bering Land Bridge twenty or more thousand years ago, the rocks atop Mount St. Helens had been lying there for at least thirty thousand years and perhaps a lot more. Experts differ on the mountain's age. Native American descendants of the early humanoids knew the mountain either as Loowit (mountain given beauty by spirits) or as Louwala-Clough (fire mountain). Loowit was formed when a tectonic plate known as the Juan de Fuca plate subducted under the North American plate, shoving up a new mountain. The earth's belly fire began to find new channels upward. Captain George Vancouver, a man of Dutch descent who gained fame as an English seaman and explorer of the Pacific Northwest, christened the mountain with its English name in honor of his friend Baron St. Helens. Vancouver's mappings were done primarily in the 1780s, a couple of decades before the Americans Meriwether Lewis and William Clark came on their Corps of Discovery Expedition from the east.

Based on charcoal dating around Loowit, volcan- ologists believe there was a large eruption in 1800, just before Lewis and Clark came calling in 1803. Other large eruptions were dated to 2335 BC, 1855 BC, 1675 BC, and then two in the AD 1480s. All told, there were twenty-three eruptions prior to an unusually active period beginning in 1831, when the mountain upchucked nine times in twenty- six years. Depending on which expert is doing the testing, the first eruptions began forty thousand—or perhaps eighty thousand—years ago. The 1980 hemorrhage is by far the best known to the modern world, since it came in the era of mass communications. It followed a nap of a hundred twenty-three years. All the world saw a twelve-hundred-foot section of vertical terra firma form a bulge, grow by five feet a day, and suddenly become Jell-O. Fifty-seven people died. There were warnings and voluntary evacuations, but many stayed within the mountain's reach because the USGS couldn't predict the north flank lump would become a lateral blast that would pulverize two hundred twenty square miles. The area was literally sterilized. For decades, nonnative bacteria prospered because their controlling species were incinerated.

After the 1980 eruption, ash disposal was an enormous problem not well covered in the media feeding frenzy. Hundreds of thousands of tons of the gritty residue lay on the surrounding countryside and in the many lakes and streams. The mess was scooped into thousands upon thousands of truckloads and dumped into landfills, ditches, and bodies of water where it would eventually be carried by rain and current to the sea.

A substantial impoundment known as Spirit Lake could be walked across. It was completely covered with floating wood because the eruption blasted innumerable trees into random chunks. Years later, the logs still blanketed the lake's surface.

An exotic formation of lava cooled and dried into a hollow tube a human could walk through. The tunnel became known as Ape Cave due to Sasquatch sightings nearby. A growth unofficially called Cave Slime abounded on the lava tube walls. The substance was composed of an algae-bacteria crust so delicate it died immediately when touched. The slime shimmered when a flashlight shone upon it because of its remarkable moisture-holding property. Bats, moths, and little mousy creatures called pikas fed on the slime and flourished. Locals thought Bigfoot had a taste for it, as well.

Loowit always trembled before she hurled, and right now she was shaking her hips and seismically wide awake. Periods of sharp jolts measuring up to magnitude 3.3 occurred as often as three or four times a minute up and down the flanks of her 1.6-mile height. She was growing taller as the oozing magma built a new dome. No one could say for sure what would happen, but every living creature was on alert.

28

WAPATOO—BIGFOOT POTATOES

Sasquatch gave Loowit a wide berth when she was misbehaving. During normal times, there was exceptional berry picking and deer hunting near her, but when steam and ash began to hiss, every creature capable of leaving had enough sense to pull up stakes. On Saturday, as Jake and Jess relaxed at home, the Sasquatch family groups were closer to each other than usual because of the volcano. The twenty-three in the mother cave to the east fashioned an uncommon forum. Sasquatch sightings were often related to weather events like rain or snowstorms. Meteorological rumblings stirred up wildlife as the creatures moved about to find shelter. Now, besides the El Niño rains, the mountain's rumbling was distressing the animals.

Separated from the cave group, three Sasquatch were wading slowly through the shallows of a clear stream nearby. They were gathering wapatoo, the wild arrowhead root that grew in abundance under the water. They felt for the wapatoo bulbs with their big feet and toes and tossed them onto the bank after peeling away the bitter stalk. Pioneering humans had also cooked and eaten the roots, claiming they tasted like potatoes. The Sasquatch ate them raw after giving them a rub with a handful of spicy juniper berries, their version of a recipe. One of the creatures tossed a wapatoo bulb and looked to the sky, where a chevron formation of Canadian geese glided noisily overhead. The Bigfoot watched carefully for a moment, and a trace of smile crossed his lips.

The enormous creatures wading in the stream were also fishing with their hands, keeping one eye on the water for fish that might swim close enough to be grabbed up just like the grizzly bears did it, or scooped to the bank with a lightning-quick motion. They knew nothing about the diffraction of light but over the millennia had developed an uncanny ability to judge where a fish was actually located in the water instead of where it seemed to be. One of the creatures snagged a large salmon and slit its belly open with a sharp fingernail not unlike a claw. The fish's guts flopped into the water at the same moment it wriggled free from the big hand. The Bigfoot watched with amazement as the gutless salmon swished its tail and swam away, unaware that it was dead.

Farther north, some two hundred miles above Vancouver in an eight-million-acre Canadian national park called Great Bear Rainforest, the largest temperate rain forest on Earth, Sasquatch had taught themselves to fish for volume. They hoisted thirty-foot dead logs into the salmon-rich streams and formed them into a V. The channeled fish could only escape downstream through a small opening, where the Sasquatch waited to scoop and grab.

Most of the creatures hunted and gathered at night. Deer were the main prey. They enjoyed an impressive success rate at surrounding a resting deer, then closing in quietly. By the time the deer alerted, it was usually too late. A big foot was stamped and the deer ran away from the sound, directly toward another Sasquatch that would sweep the animal off its feet and snap its neck in one swift motion. The hunting party would then slice open the belly with flint rocks, remove the viscera, and consume the raw liver and heart on the spot. They carried much of the muscle meat back to their extended families for sharing. Depending on their camouflage and hunger, the meat was eaten raw or, when safe, singed over a small fire.

29

FARM—FATHER KNOWS BEST

Jake's afternoon was suffused with a bone-deep melancholy. He tried to shake off the feeling of impending doom without success. Killing the Sasquatch and suffering the sting of charges from Jessica's father had plunged him into dispiritedness. He couldn't stay in the present; things he'd long tried to forget were fresh again. "They found a lump," she had said. "I'm scared."

He remembered taking her in his arms and holding her tightly, too tightly. He remembered the tears that flooded his eyes and how he hid them from her, thinking she needed him to be strong. "Let's don't get ahead of ourselves," he'd said finally. "You're young, and you're healthy. Maybe it's nothing. Whatever it is, we'll take care of it. They say it's serious. If it's serious, we'll beat it." He knew he was building a little nest of deception for both of them to retreat into, and he didn't like it. He wanted to scream. He wanted to run outside and curse God and ram his fist through a tree. The feeling flashed through his nervous system that maybe the illness couldn't be beaten. He wanted desperately to be wrong. Her stomach pains and sleepless nights had troubled him from the beginning. He was physically ill when her monthly flow suddenly stopped. He wanted to bellow like a rutting elk, but he couldn't. He hid the tears and told her, "Just hold on to me." Later, when he was alone, the dam burst. He cracked his ring finger sucker-punching a door. He allowed himself to moan like a mother crying over an injured child in a dusty village a world away. Jessica sensed his dark mood and tried to be of good cheer. Her instinct was to help. "Hey there, Mr. Man," she sang, "don't think I can't tell when you're in a funk." She approached his chair by the fire. She placed her fingers on either side of his neck and began to massage. "Would this help? I know Allie's in the room with us. Do you want to talk about her? You know I don't mind." Jess's rubdown reached Jake's shoulder blades with her thumbs pushing firmly. His shoulders squared and his head fell back. He released a groan of pleasure. She roamed outward until each hand surrounded a shoulder, then pressed her fingers into his baseball-tenderized rotator cuffs and made circular movements.

"Gawdalmighty," Jake rasped. "You are good. You sure you didn't work in one of those naughty massage parlors? And, yes, that helps. What did I do to deserve you?"

"Who said you deserve me?"

The iceberg began to melt. He grinned at her. "I don't like it one bit that you can read my mind. That's dangerous. But I love you for not fretting when the past comes back."

"If you didn't think about her, you wouldn't be the man I know you to be. Then you certainly wouldn't deserve me." She continued the deep massage of his upper body. He relaxed. "You know, both of us are going to get old and lumpy. We're going to have fights about the smallest things. One of your knees will give out, and I just might swell up so ugly and fat I don't have fingerprints. My hair will turn white. I'll get ingrown toenails, and you'll have Don King ear hair. But this Sasquatch thing will pass away. The world will go on."

Jake reached back to take her hands. "Lumpy?" he said. "I doubt the part about you getting lumpy or ugly. That'll never happen."

Jess sighed dramatically. "Yes, I know. Purity endures . . . with maybe a little nip and tuck from the surgeon to help."

"If you want that, you'll have it. But plastic surgery would be for you, not for me. Maybe we'll find a way to grow old gracefully."

"Sure we will. We'll pop pills and inject genes and eat tree bark and exercise like maniacs. We won't be old until we're a hundred and fifty."

"And if that doesn't work, the hell with it. We'll grow old together. You keep massaging me, I won't mind clipping your ingrown toenails."

"Deal," Jess said. "We'll avoid the old saw about loving the idea of a person rather than the actual person. We won't need illusions. But it won't be easy. Who was that gnarly poet who said, 'Love is a dog from hell'? We'll prove him wrong."

Jake turned in his chair and took her by the wrists. He gently pulled her over the back of the chair and into his lap. She relented willingly and squirmed to help. He kissed her lightly at first and gave her lower lip a grazing bite. She wiggled sensuously in his lap. As he pulled his face away from hers, she gave his cheek a kitty lick with the tip of her tongue and giggled when he pulled her closer and kissed her full on the mouth. "Hey," she said. "I like how you get over the blues. Is it just me, or is that fire getting warmer?"

"Something's warmer around here, you luscious little girl. Here, I'll help you out of that sweater. That must be why you're warm."

A phone rang. They paused in their nuzzling to listen. The chime of the choral movement from Beethoven's Ninth Symphony identified the call as coming from Jess's cell phone across the room. "I'll let it go," she said. "Bad timing."

"Maybe you should answer. It might be your dad."

"Do you want me to?"

"Of course I don't want you to. You feel wonderful, and you smell good, and you're kinda cute. But you probably should."

"OK."

Jake stared at the fire as she crossed the room and answered. He could tell it was her dad. A series of silences punctuated with *yes, no, good grief, OK, right, sure, thanks very much, bye* disclosed little about the chat. When she returned, she stood in front of him with her back to the fire.

"How's that for timing?" she asked.

"Fathers always know when their beautiful girls are about to get in trouble. What did he want?"

"He assumed we were together and wanted us to know what took place at the courthouse. He noticed we weren't there."

"So what happened?"

"He didn't say much. He made up an excuse for the meeting by talking about St. Helens. He said the people who came were upset with him because they were all hearing Sasquatch rumors and wanted to know more."

"Why didn't he tell them? I thought that was the point. I've been worried sick that everyone would know."

"Here comes the good part. He got a phone call from the White House. The president asked him to keep it quiet. A special military unit is coming late this evening or in the morning. He said these guys are set up to handle stuff like this."

"Oh, great. Yeah, I'll bet they handle it. I can see the helmets and black helicopters now."

"Dad said the president told him they're discreet and low-key, but I see what you mean. He's told no one—not even my mother, because that's what the president requested. He's asking Oscar and Eldo and you and me to do the same."

"Fine with me. I wasn't planning on telling anyone."

Jess moved away from the fire and sat on the arm of Jake's chair. She was quiet for a moment.

Jake said, "There must be something else, judging from the look in your eyes."

"Is it that obvious? Looks like you read my mind as well as I read yours. Here's the strangest part of all. He asked us to dinner tonight, just him and Mom and the two of us. I said yes. I'm thinking I should have checked with you first. How do you feel about it?"

"This day couldn't get any weirder. Your dad charges me with murder and you with being an accessory. Then he calls and invites us to dinner. Why would we go?"

Jess put her hand on Jake's knee and rubbed absentmindedly. "I get the feeling he's having second thoughts.

That's why I said yes. Maybe with the president's call and these men coming here, he wants to drop the charges and clean the slate."

"Can he do that?"

"Yes, he can. It's up to him."

"Well, if he's inviting us over socially, that seems like progress. Unless it's a trap, and he's decided to shoot me."

"He definitely was trying to reach out."

"That has to be good news. We should go. But my stress level is rising again. You may have to go back to work on me." Jake smiled up at her, as she was perched on the chair arm with a nearly unbuttoned sweater. He held up his index finger and wiggled a seductive, come-here gesture. "Now, where were we?"

30

SHERIFF—ELDO PONDERS

Eldo reached for the pint of Old Forester in his bottom desk drawer. He set it on the desk next to the accordion folder of Sasquatch reports, unscrewed the cap, and took a generous swig from the bottle. He puffed his cheeks and swished the hundred-proof bourbon in his mouth like he might start to gargle. The fire flashed up through his nose, so he tilted his head back and swallowed the liquor in one gulp. The raw, potent, woody flavor encouraged him to shake his head before exhaling slowly. As far as most Aurorians knew, Eldo Throckmorton was a teetotaler. He encouraged that perception since there was an election every four years, and he'd been unopposed the last two times. When Eldo took a drink, he usually did it alone. The exceptions were his wife and Tal O'Reilly.

Eldo swept his big hand into the folder like a scoop shovel and emerged with a clutch of newspaper clippings, magazine articles, and Internet postings, all on the same subject. He fanned them onto his desk and began to peruse. A Florida woman claimed to have spotted an eight-foot-tall creature with two-inch brown hair covering its body. It was one day after a hurricane. According to the article, such incidents had been reported in the South for more than two hundred years, with seventy-five sightings in the past twenty years alone. This subtropical monster was a relative of Bigfoot known as the skunk ape because of its alleged stench. The woman said she saw it stooped over a ditch collecting frogs, and that it had enormous lips the texture of a dog's paw.

A longer article from a national magazine dissected a small town in Oklahoma nicknamed Bigfootsville. The town was surrounded by dense woods, streams, and rugged country. Sightings were commonplace. A large ape or ape man traipsed through the woods and was once spotted crossing an open field. A few locals produced blurry pictures and shaky videos that were interpreted according to the predisposition of the viewer. Deer were found slashed open and eviscerated. A local policeman testified, convincingly, that he saw a creature cross a rural road he was patrolling and easily jump-step over a five-foot fence. Night-vision cameras and sensitive audio recorders were set up during stakeouts, but they produced nothing conclusive.

Eldo's files contained reports of sightings from several places around the United States and abroad, including the famous Abominable Snowman of the Himalayas. Eldo pulled his chair closer to the desk and leaned forward. He shuffled through the clippings like they were face cards and he was looking for a king. He leaned back and let his gaze drift upward to the ceiling fan that hadn't worked for years. For a moment, he felt as docile as a smoked bee.

Despite his effort to avoid it, Eldo was thinking about Tom Ward. Tom was the only deputy Eldo ever hired. He kept two others on the payroll after being elected. Tom came aboard after Tal suggested the county was growing and Eldo could use extra help. Tom was a deer hunter from a tiny burg ten miles away. Everyone liked him. After some training, he was a good deputy and better friend. Eldo enjoyed having him around. Tom and Tal were the only Aurorians who got away with needling Eldo about his full name, Eldorado Funder Throckmorton.

Then Tom was killed. He went hunting in a remote area and didn't come back. Eldo had a general idea where to look for his deer stand, which hung twenty feet up a hemlock tree. Tom, or what was left of him, lay at the bottom of the tree. His body was ripped apart. An autopsy was inconclusive. The theory evolved that Tom fell from the tree and knocked himself out and a bear found him. No one could successfully explain why his rifle had fired one round and was found snapped in two. Or why Tom's remains weren't eaten. "Jesus God," Eldo said to the ceiling fan. He took another generous pull from the bourbon bottle before putting it back in the drawer. He looked again at his pile of Bigfoot clippings and then out the window. "Jesus H. Holy God."

31

BILLY'S FLOOD—THE SPY BREAKS FREE

Saturday at Billy Lasswell's house wasn't pretty. His dad was hungover and spoiling for trouble. Still irritated about the basement flooding, Edgar departed for Hee-Haw's but commanded Billy to deal with the problem. The drain was clogged and not removing any water from the concrete floor. His father had assigned the seemingly endless task of collecting muddy water with a plastic bucket, hauling it up the rickety stairs, and hurling it through the propped-open back door.

"Don't even think about quittin' till all that water's bailed and the floor's cleaned up," Edgar growled.

The boy hauled and hurled for a half hour, but the water level didn't seem to move. Billy wanted nothing more in life than to finish his chore so he could sprint to Chuck's house and get back on the Internet with his Sasquatch story. Chuck believed him. Chuck's mother and father might even believe him. But his own dad told him to shut up about it.

"That's enough," he said. "Leave it be, or I'll blister you. People will think you're crazy. Get down there and get that water out."

Billy would have been flabbergasted to hear his father say "my boy don't lie" to the tavern regulars that afternoon. Billy sat on the rickety stairs and appraised his situation. He stared at the standing water until he pictured the floor drain and where it might lie. It was Billy's eureka moment. He had been trying to think of a better way to remove the water. He removed the worn out tennis shoes he'd been ruining by slogging through the water and began to wade with purpose. He used his bare feet to tap in every direction as he closed in on where the drain might be. He was off by a yard but soon felt it. He squatted to explore the floor with his fingers and felt the drain cover as if reading Braille, noting the one screw holding the cover on with the other screw missing. He fetched a Phillips screwdriver from the workbench and relocated the drain. Billy loosened the screw and removed the mud-caked cover, a six-inch plastic circle with a series of small holes that were stopped up by dirt as hard as plaster. But removing the drain cap had no effect on the standing water, so he twisted his hand into the open drainpipe and dug his fingers like mole claws into a disgusting mess.

"Ewww," Billy said quietly as he dug out a wad of gunk and flopped it into his bucket. For a second he thought the water began to flow and then stopped, so he dug some more, then more until he couldn't reach any farther into the drainpipe, which angled away from the floor. He attacked the angle with a length of heavy wire he rustled up, pushing and pulling it through the pipe. Billy heard a burp and saw a bubble. He stuck his bare foot over the opening. Water gushed down the pipe and washed away the caked mud and grunge, gaining momentum.

"Well, yee-haw," Billy said matter-of-factly.

A few more reams with his wire, and the water was beaten. A hosing of the floor and some broom work and he would be on his way to Chuck's.

Billy's persistence in finding a way to overcome his problem allowed him to escape being stuck in the dungeon, bailing water the entire afternoon. Had that occurred, the young man might not have become Dr. William Lasswell, the leading cryptozoologist in the world.

32

HEE-HAW'S 3—LOCAL YARNS

The proprietor was in perfect pitch. The tap opened early and flowed freely. Hee-Haw was an impassioned connoisseur of old-timey, rural expressions. He worked them in every chance he got—and then some. Most of the time they made sense. Sometimes he tried too hard. Hee-Haw preached that television was causing everyone to sound the same, robbing the country of its variety of accents and homespun language. "We need to save these old sayings," he liked to say, "but that's about as easy as lickin' honey off a thorn tree."

As usual, the barroom conversation percolated across a spectrum of topics that ran the gamut from serious to colorful to mundane. The Sasquatch was the overriding subject of the day, in particular whether it was true that a Bigfoot cadaver was lying somewhere nearby. Tal O'Reilly's obfuscation at the courthouse had fueled a general irritation among the tavern crowd. They felt they were being duped. Tal's pretext of volcanic ash warnings resulted in the conclusion that something secret was afoot, something that warranted a group excursion to the funeral home. The beery wisdom by four o'clock stipulated a call to Oscar before the troupe marched to his building. They would ask him to open up for a look. They would use a crowbar if he refused. Meanwhile, the bar talk gathered momentum.

"You just can't get better beer than this Oly," observed a middle-aged patron sporting a salt-and-pepper soul patch and goatee, "because you can't find better water than we have in Washington."

"Actually, Oly is made in L.A.," a college student corrected. "They sold out to Pabst a long time ago and didn't tell us when they moved. They ran an ad campaign saying what a pleasant, light beer it was at the same time the Pabst brewery was changing it to a heavy, European-style. They confused everybody. Younger people were trying it, expecting something light-tasting, like Coors, and then thinking something was wrong with it. Now it's just cheap beer."

"'Fraid he's right," Hee-Haw chimed. "That don't make it bad beer. These college boys are usually dumber'n a barrel of hair, and if brains were dynamite they couldn't blow their nose. But he's right on this one. Oly sold out a long time ago. Hell, you old guys are supposed to know a few things. You know as much about beer as a dog knows about Sunday. I will say you're pretty good at drinking it, though."

Two women sat in a booth of red vinyl, their heads scrunched close together as if they were discussing classified documents. One was a fortyish black woman with light skin and her hair pulled into a short ponytail. The other, who was speaking, was similar in age but had the impersonal aspect of someone familiar with trouble. She had platinum-blonde hair with dark roots. Her makeup was painted on thick in a failed attempt to cover crow's feet and skin that had seen too much sunlight.

"I love Eddie," she said. "I really do love him. But I can't leave my husband. I won't leave him as long as he don't beat me or cut me. That sounds dumb. What's wrong with me? I also got a friend from high school lives down in Florida. He's been calling me, and I know he wants me to move down there with him. That's what I oughta do. But I won't. I don't ever do the thing that would work out."

"I hear you," the other woman said. "I've been trying really hard not to cheat on my boyfriend, even though the way he treats me, I should. Finally I figured something out. If I don't shave my legs, I won't cheat on him. But if I go out to a bar with smooth legs and have a few drinks, I can't be sure what I'll do."

At an adjacent table a woman who might have been forty or sixty spoke quietly to her husband of many years. "Won't you at least try to talk to me about Vietnam?" she said with a hint of sadness. It was not a new conversation for them. "You hardly ever say anything. Maybe it would help me understand your moods if you'd tell me what you're thinking. Did you have to kill anyone? Wouldn't it help to talk about it?"

"Yes and no." He was a tall man with a lean and angular build and quiet comportment who despised his job selling insurance. "You act like I want to talk about it, but can't. That's not it. I don't want to talk about it or even think about it. What's the point? I'd rather talk about what we'll have for supper, or whether our son will ever finish college. The world may be insane, but our little corner of it doesn't have to be."

"But you still dream about it. You wake up trying to catch your breath. It bothers me a lot, especially when you won't tell me anything."

"OK. I understand what you're saying. But after this, we talk about garlic cheese bread. I've wanted to avoid telling you about the dream, but I'll tell you if you insist. I don't think you'll like it. You have to remember you're the one insisting. You tell me what to do. Are you sure you want to hear it?"

She paused for a moment. "Yes, I'm sure I do. It can't be worse than my imagination."

"Even when I say you won't like it? You still want to hear? Are you absolutely sure?"

"Yes. Yes, I'm sure. You're scaring me."

"OK. The thing is . . ." He tried to think how to begin. There was no good way. He laid his right index finger alongside his right nostril and scratched. "The thing is, I might have a daughter over there. I can't be sure. One night, a young Vietnamese woman I knew told me she was having my baby. Her name was Lam Thi Mai, and she was quite young. I already said that. She was about sixteen, at the most. Two days later, I was sent to the other end of the country. Two weeks later, I stepped on the punji stick—you know about that—and was on my way home. I didn't see her again, but I never forgot."

The wife sat still and stared at her fingernails. She had pushed for the truth, the reality behind the curtain, and a wave of regret flushed through her. Her hands trembled. An unfamiliar emotion boiled up, followed by the familiar feeling she didn't know him at all. "Why would you say it was a daughter?" she said. "She couldn't have known the gender when she told you that."

"Because of the dream you wanted to know about. She didn't say a gender, but my dream has added that. It started a year or two after I came back, before I met you. I'm in a little Vietnamese hooch, and a baby girl is born. She looks like an Asian version of me. Over the years since then, Mai has stayed exactly the same. But the little girl ages in the dream. She became a teenager and then stopped aging. She looks at me and holds out a hand. I wake up with my heart pounding. As soon as I'm awake, I know it's not real and I'm fine. It might be weeks or months before the dream returns. I thought it would eventually go away, but recently it's gotten more frequent. The girl is beautiful in the dream, and I feel wonderful when I see her. Then a woman's voice asks, 'Where is your father?' The girl says, 'My father is dead.'"

There was silence at the table, long enough that it became awkward. The man regretted his disclosure. It was his private version of himself as a younger man, the person he'd been a long time ago. He'd never spoken of it. The dream was his connection to the past, to a time of confusion, pride, bitterness, elation, dread, and horror—all rolled together into one insoluble puzzle, his war experience. Like many Vietnam veterans, he didn't believe the war had been a mistake. He believed if America had asserted itself instead of wallowing in self-doubt, especially in light of Communism's subsequent implosion, Vietnam today might be a cornerstone of Asian freedom. He read and appreciated recent books that analyzed the Vietnam experience, books that concluded Uncle Sam was the good guy. He thought about the remarkable Vietnamese people and how grateful they were for the protection GIs gave them from brutal North Vietnamese invaders and their Vietcong puppets. He didn't accept the notion the United States "lost" the war in Vietnam, but believed the media and naïve protesters caused a breakdown of will. He thought of the millions of ordinary Vietnamese tortured, suppressed, and murdered by the North Vietnamese Communists after the war. It made him physically ill. He thought about Lam Thi Mai and his throat tightened.

He wanted his wife to say something. She didn't. He felt the ground between them shift. He took a drink from his glass of beer and set it down with an emphatic clunk. "You wanted to know. Now you know. Can we please talk about supper?"

Across the room in a booth near the bar, two men needled a third about his first colonoscopy, scheduled for Monday. "Don't worry about it, T-Bone," a man named Beverly Porter said to the victim. "You may like getting reamed with a fire hose. You and the doc will be legally married in Arkansas."

"Hey, you and him might move to Arkansas," the other man chimed in. He puckered his mouth into an O and puffed his cheeks. He looked like a pink balloon. "They still point at planes there. You'd fit right in."

"You say T-Bone would fit in?" The speaker was Hee-Haw, delivering a round and grinning ear to ear. "I'm taking up for the poor man. You two are about as smart as the old boy who wouldn't give a dime to see the Resurrection. You wouldn't walk a mile to see a pissant eat a bale of hay. T-Bone, when you wallow with pigs, expect to get dirty. It's these two oughta move to Arkansas. Except when the rednecks down in Dogpatch find out ol' Porter's name is Beverly, he might be on his way back to Washington in a hurry."

"Yeah, yeah," Bev said. He spun his beer glass and watched the bubbles. "You always come back to the name game. Can't you guys think up something new?" Beverly was numb to jokes about his name.

"Albert," T-Bone said to Hee-Haw, "forget these losers, and bring me a hot dog, a cheeseburger, and some fries with gravy. I don't start my fasting until tomorrow, and I want to be as full of crap as my buddies here. That should get me started."

"Praise the Lord," Hee-Haw exulted, raising his arm in a mock salute. "You can't live a life without suffering, but T-Bone knows life is easier when you plow around the stump."

33

OL' VIC 2—LOOK WHO'S COMING TO DINNER

"I'm not complaining, but you have to admit this is weird," Jake said. He and Jess were dressing for a casual dinner. "Your father charges us with a major crime because I accidentally shot a creature that doesn't exist. Now we're having dinner with him."

"I can't explain," Jess said. "Impossible things are happening. How could it make sense? You didn't mention the call from the leader of the free world and his SWAT team on the way."

"Right. Just give me a summary. I can tell I need to shut up and go along. But what do I say to someone who doesn't like me, wants to make me a criminal, and wants me to stay away from someone I love?"

"I'll try, but don't expect me to clear up what I don't understand myself." She coached Jake as they drove to Ol' Vic. She took a guess about the dinner invitation. She said her father was emotional and spontaneous. Perhaps he was having second thoughts about the charges. The dinner might be a way for him to learn more about what happened in the woods and whether he went off half-cocked. Maybe her mother found out what was happening and confronted Tal, she conjectured, or perhaps the president's call drastically changed the landscape of the situation. Maybe Tal realized he was fanning the flames, and with the feds on the way, he needed to slow things down. "Dad likes control. He hates loose ends. He might see the situation getting away from him, so he wants allies. Maybe he's started thinking like you—that we're into uncharted water and need to sort things out before the situation overwhelms us. But you asked what you should say to him. You know that answer."

"I did? I do?"

"Yes. Just be your charming self and say what you think. I wouldn't have it any other way. You know I'll be in your corner. One thing's for sure, if he's trying to clear the air and you can forgive him his trespasses, you two would enjoy being wine geeks together."

34

COPSE—THEY WANT THE BODY

In late afternoon as the sun dives to the horizon and gathering darkness signals the cycle's turn, winds calm and the air goes gentle. Most of the time, that is. When an active volcano and El Niño intersect, all bets are off.

In the higher elevations above Aurora, another rain organized itself and marched downhill. The spring sunshine wasn't without aspiration, but its warmth was foreclosed by a thickening cloud cover. In the gloomy half-light, Mount St. Helens's glow of burning ash coalesced with throbbing steam and water vapor to look ever more like a menacing chunk of hellfire pushed upward by an irresistible force. The rain and superheated air around the volcano formed a complex inversion layer. The usual west-to-east wind pattern was amended by unseen forces to blow from the north, sending the volcano's ashy waste toward Aurora. The stout wind bowed branches and was damp with the smell of rainwater. Giant trees rustled and scratched, sounding like paper being balled. Raindrops piggybacked on pieces of ash hissing down through the canopy like handfuls of gravel pitched into a puddle. In the days of myth, thousands of years gone, humans believed white-winged angels might take them by the hand and away from trouble.

There were no angels in Aurora. At Hee-Haw's Tavern, beer-drinking men watched a TV set that exhibited the talking head of a man in Seattle pointing at a map with red arrows. The arrows predicted the path of volcanic smoke and ash plume, give or take. The well-spoken man said a "light basting" of dust was all that would happen, and that people should stay indoors for the evening.

At an elevation of four thousand feet above Aurora and to the east, safely away from Loowit's grumbling and spitting, the unprecedented convention of Sasquatch continued near the mother cave. In the fifteen or so millennia the outcast hominids had been wandering and hiding in the North American Northwest, barely surviving as a species and doing that only thanks to a brawny body and clever-enough brain, there had been little reason to congregate. They'd survived all that time by not congregating, not drawing attention.

However, congregating they were, in a dense copse of stunted trees and thick underbrush near the cave. There were thirty Sasquatch in a variety of shapes, sizes, tints, genders, and ages, all drawn together by their high-pitched communication whistles. Enormous males shared the rocky outcrop with slightly smaller females, some of them pregnant. The females presided over the smaller ones, who ranged in age from chimp-sized newborns to energetic adolescents nearly the size of Clydesdales.

They sniffed each other through gaping nostrils in a mannerly and genteel fashion, heads tilted back and eyes closed in apparent satisfaction. There was no sign of male aggression or territorial jealousy, as might have been expected in a gathering of wild creatures. There was a serious effort to communicate. They didn't possess words that an observer might have divined as such. The grunts and snorts and clicks were accompanied by decisive gestures with lips and eyebrows and heads moving in animation. Colossal fingers were pointed. Mammoth hands were slapped against hairy arms and chests. Certain gestures and vocalizations were repeated by others as if to signal agreement.

The male shot in the shoulder by Jake, recognizable by the mud poultice smeared over his wound—front and back, entry and exit—took a leadership role in the aggregation. The others paid particular attention to him. They understood. Clearly, moving a hand up and down chopping the air signaled the affirmative. The posturing and chatter continued for twenty minutes with many of the creatures contributing. It ended when several of the males followed the leader in making the up-and-down arm motion with clenched fists while baring and clacking their teeth.

A few older males and most of the female and young Sasquatch left the thicket to move uphill toward the cave. The sixteen that remained, the fittest and most bellicose, turned and strode purposefully downhill. The group included three females. They covered the ground and forest floor with a wide, high-octane gait that would get them quickly to their destination: Aurora.

35

JOURNALISTS 2—BAD DRIVING

Somewhere in Northern California, Ashok's nap was rudely interrupted. Kenzo had persevered through several hours of mind numbing freeway driving while Ashok relaxed, but when the wheels slipped off the pavement and weeds slapped the Toyota's quarter panels, both men were instantly awake.

"I damn hell sorry," Kenzo said after jerking the car back on the roadway. "Buku sleepy. Shit, damn, hell, bastard, suicide, piss. No think I stay awake longer."

"What time is it?" Ashok said. "I slept and now it's dark. Where are we? Oh, there's a sign that says *Eureka*—like Archimedes in his bathtub. I gather I need to discover something too, such as how to drive this car. According to our little map, we're close to Oregon. Pull over, Kenzo, and I'll drive."

"Promise no kill me? I too tired to worry."

The I-5 traffic on Saturday was light by local standards, but there were still plenty of cars on the road. Ashok moved into his lane slowly, accelerating carefully to a blistering forty-five miles an hour. Kenzo watched closely for a few minutes, until Ashok seemed to have the hang of staying in his lane. Kenzo laid his head back and was soon out cold, his mouth wide open and gargling an odd rattle, like a motorboat needing a tune-up.

Ashok hadn't told Kenzo, but his taxi-driving cousin in Delhi had given him basic instruction. *This is nothing. I am a man who has driven a taxi in India*, he thought, taking a deep breath to slow his heartbeat.

Kenzo's audio accompaniment increased in volume. It brought to mind a dentist's evacuation sink.

It doesn't matter when we get there as long as we arrive safely, Ashok reminded himself. *It's odd that they drive on the right here.*

He looked at the dashboard. He was up to forty-nine. Despite the light traffic, a steady parade whizzed by to his left. The passing drivers screwed their heads around to see if Ashok was a little old lady. *It doesn't matter. Sunday is just as good as Saturday.*

36

OL' VIC 3—WINE AND DINNER AS THE BEASTS APPROACH

Jessica's mother met Jessica at the door with an outsized hello and kiss on the cheek. Now into her sixties, friends and family still called her Ruthie due to her youthful appearance. She found it took effort to retain the fine-boned and freckled good looks of her younger self, the same beauty she passed to her daughter. Things sagged. Her skin caused trouble, her eyes pooched, the lines on her face deepened. But she dutifully scrubbed and spackled and creamed and combed it all into submission. She was a lovely woman. Tal was three steps behind her, the picture of cordiality and earnestness in his welcome.

Standing beside Jess, Jake felt on display. His mind raced. After a moment he noticed he was the only one feeling uneasy, so he forced himself to relax.

Tal worked hard to put the group at ease. "Hi, Jess," he said with willful calm. "Good evening, Jake. I'm really glad you came. May I say right off the bat I'm sorry about this morning? I must have seemed aggressive."

"To say the least," Jess said.

"Jake, come in. Make yourself at home. I mean that," Tal continued. "They call this place Old Victoria, or Ol' Vic, because of all the gingerbread and gewgaws." Tal paused. "I'm sure it feels strange to be here for dinner after this morning. I hope both of you will let me try to explain."

Jake looked up at the intricately carved crown moldings. He smiled and said, "Interesting." He was determined to be friendly to Tal, while keeping his distance.

Ruthie looked puzzled by her husband's awkward behavior. She took Jake by the arm and led him into the house while Jess and Tal trailed along.

The conversation was polite but tinged with a sense of formality. Their socializing wasn't spontaneous. Tal tried hard, making small talk about the mountain and the inconvenient ash cloud now circling into town. It took Ruthie and the Honor Post to thaw the proceedings. They were standing near the stairs when Ruthie said, "Jessica, you remember this newel-post. As far as I know, not one of you three kids ever told a lie after swearing on it."

"Are you kidding? No one could ever lie on the sacred Honor Post. Come to think of it, who started that?"

"It was Ewing," Tal offered. "He was in grade school, and he had a buddy nicknamed Toad. I can't remember his real name. They're the ones who got it started. They were always making up tall tales to tell each other. They decided they needed a way to separate truth from fiction."

"Jess has mentioned the Honor Post," Jake offered, trying to join in. "I didn't know the details."

Jess took Jake's arm as they walked past the stairway into an old-fashioned parlor. A bottle of Beaux Frères Pinot Noir from Oregon sat breathing in a crystal decanter.

"Those boys would put each other on the Honor Post. If they put their hand on it, they were bound by honor to tell nothing but the truth. It was like swearing on the Bible, only stronger. It stuck. They wouldn't violate the Honor Post, no matter what. Before long they didn't need to actually touch it. All they had to do was ask, 'Honor Post?' If the other one swore on it you could bet whatever he said was true. They spread it to the rest of our family. I have to tell you, Jake, it came in pretty handy at times."

"I can imagine," Jake said. "That's an interesting tradition. Now I can use it on Jessica."

Jess giggled and swatted Jake on the arm. "You don't need it," she said, raising her chin to a holier-than-thou angle and channeling George Washington. "I cannot tell a lie." She paused. "And now that we've explained it, you're also bound by the Honor Post."

"Fair enough," Jake agreed.

Tal moved to the wine and poured generously into Riedel glasses from Austria, shaped especially for Pinot Noir. They were wide and round at the bottom and smaller at the top, to focus the wine's stunning nose of black cherries, smoke, and spice. The foursome swirled and sniffed appreciatively.

"I hate wine snob speeches," Tal said. "But if you'll indulge me for a minute?" He offered a knowledgeable tutelage about the wine's vintage year and growing season in the Willamette Valley. He said rough early weather allowed only the hardiest grapes to survive, but September sunshine made them yield concentrated wine with flavors of dark fruit, vanilla, and mushrooms. "Let's try it," Tal said. "But no toasts. That's a distraction."

The four dutifully sipped, swishing the wine along the back and sides of their tongues, and then swallowed and inhaled. No one said a word. Their expressions suggested they might have swallowed a magic elixir, or sipped from the fountain of youth.

"Mmm," Jessica hummed. "That is intense. What do you think, Jake?"

"Simply outstanding. I even liked the speech. My blackberries are packed with flavor, but this concentrates the experience. Thank you."

Tal looked happy. "It is my pleasure to pour it," he said, opening a second bottle for the decanter. "I've heard good things about your farm, Jake. Jess told us you're interested in wine and possibly growing wine grapes one of these days. Tell us more about what you're doing and how you got started."

"I moved here and bought the property because . . . well, you might say I was at the bottom of an abyss back in Missouri. I became a widower at a young age because of a runaway cancer."

"We know about that, Jake," Ruthie said solemnly. "We're so sorry it happened."

"Thank you. Everyone here has been very kind. I needed to get away from it. I could've ended up anywhere. For a while I thought about losing myself in a big city, maybe Chicago or New York."

"You'd have been lost, all right, living on concrete," Jess teased.

"The big trees in this part of the country fascinate me. I visited out here during a trip to Portland after she died. I got on the blue highways and then the dirt roads into the Douglas firs. I ended up spending a few extra days. I talked to a realtor—at Hee-Haw's, naturally—and he showed me the farm. That was it. I moved a month later."

"What are you growing out there?" Tal asked. "And what do you do with it?"

Ruthie brought out a silver tray of Parmesan cheese puffs and Vermont sharp cheddar with toast points of sourdough.

"I didn't grow anything at first, just moped around not wanting to get out of bed. The farm was reverting to grass and weeds, and I didn't care. I started exercising—walking and then jogging. I found a patch of wild asparagus that was fabulous to eat. I came to the realization that I had a long time to live, and I needed to get it together. I stopped feeling sorry for myself."

Ruthie spoke up. "And bravo to you for that. It couldn't have been easy to move from your home and start over."

"It was self-preservation," Jake admitted. "We owned some restaurants around St. Louis, and I managed to sell them. That allowed me to come here and eventually start fixing up the property. The other thing that helped was finding my horse, Split Log. I started riding him into the big woods, and my anger and loss took on some perspective." Jake looked at his companions and scrunched his nose. "I'm sorry to ramble on. You asked what I'm growing, and I'm telling you my life's story."

"No, no. We want to hear," Tal protested. "Please go on."

"I'm growing organic vegetables and berries. We've started an orchard with hazelnuts and Rainier cherries, and I built a small tropical greenhouse to try mangosteens. No one's growing them in North America, so that makes me want to try. Everything we grow is sold in advance to restaurants in Portland and Seattle. Sometimes the chefs help me decide what to plant. We deliver everything ourselves, and this year I've found good help from two Mexican families named Delgado and Garza. They're legal immigrants originally from Guadalajara and good, hardworking people. If we need more help, they send for a brother or an uncle or a cousin, of which there seems to be an unlimited supply. The farm has kept me going. Get up each day, breathe in, breathe out, put one foot in front of the other. And there's one other important thing. I met your daughter. If I may be permitted to say so, that's the best thing that's happened to me." Jake smiled at Jess. "I hope I'm back to normal, if there is such a thing."

"Who sold you the horse?" Tal asked.

"Guy named Wayne Holmes. I found out later he had a reputation for nicking everybody he traded with."

"That's for sure. I know him. Unless he's pulled something on you, he's not happy."

"He must've thought he got me good. He called the horse 'Bird,' and I didn't ask why. Turned out when you rode him, everything was fine until he saw birds—which, of course, was about every thirty seconds. He'd spook a little and take off after the birds like he was trying to chase them. He didn't know if he was a bird dog or Seabiscuit. The first week or two it looked pretty hopeless. I'd have to yank the bit to get him stopped, but I decided I'd be as hardheaded as Bird was. He became my new project. I just kept riding him around the farm every day and tiring him out. The birds would spook him, and I'd drag him to a stop and back him up. One day I backed him into an old, dry log and stump. He kicked a couple of times and splintered the whole mess into toothpicks. His name immediately became Split Log, and I'll be darned if he didn't quit spooking on birds that same day. Cold turkey. The next day we went into the big trees, and he was cured. He just needed a job. We go out every chance we get."

"So you really don't hunt anything?" Tal said. "You just ride?"

"If I can exercise in the morning and take Splitty out in the afternoon, that's my idea of a good day." The wine was demolishing Jake's reticence.

"Then why take a gun along at all?" Tal asked with a pleasant expression. Though it might have been taken as a loaded question, Tal didn't seem to have an ulterior motive.

"Purely for protection, Mr. O'Reilly. There are bears out there and other things that may not intend to hurt you, but can make you hurt yourself trying to get away. The old rifle is a family heirloom. It belonged to my grandfather, and I carry it to honor him. I take some overnight supplies too—in case I get lost and have to sleep in the woods. That's another good reason to have a rifle."

Tal studied Jake carefully. By coincidence, the four of them tilted their wineglasses simultaneously and sipped with obvious pleasure. They nibbled at the appetizers, especially the Parmesan puffs. Tal pressed on cheerfully before any tension could return.

"I get it," he said. "If I were clomping around out there, I'd want a rifle. Maybe a bazooka. So tell me, Jake. I know we're not supposed to talk about politics or religion, but hey, one out of two isn't bad. What are your political leanings?"

Jake found it impossible not to grin at Tal's enthusiasm. The women weren't sure if he was smiling at the bazooka wisecrack or the political inquiry. "You must be good at your job, Mr. O'Reilly. I can see you get people to talk."

"Please, Jake, call me Tal. Most people are glad to talk about themselves if you ask. We understand your hesitation, but Ruthie and I would like to know as much as we can about the guy our daughter hangs out with."

———— ◆ ————

The sixteen Sasquatch were making steady progress toward Aurora as they moved down the mountain with long strides. Except for their size and hair, they might have looked like a recon patrol of soldiers. The only sounds they made were the swishing of grass and bushes as they passed. Their breathing was silent, and no attempt at communication was made.

———— ◆ ————

With Tal's urging, Jake offered a short description of his political leanings. He said he didn't think of himself as either conservative or liberal. "I don't think I fit a label. Most people make a group of one. Any time you try to pigeonhole groups of human beings, you're automatically going to be wrong."

"How so?" Tal said.

"You were asking about my grandfather's old cannon I take on my horse rides. I also have a Smith & Wesson pistol in my home. You'd assume I'd be against gun control, right? Nope. It's ridiculous to me that we sell automatic weapons and machine pistols."

"My sentiments exactly," Ruthie chimed in.

Jessica smiled knowingly at her mother warming to Jake.

"Keep going," Tal urged. "You're on a roll if Ruthie approves."

Jake nodded in Ruth's direction and said, "Where does that put me? A group of one? I try to vote for a candidate that seems to have a sense of integrity. That's not easy to find or identify. Sometimes I think wanting to go into politics should automatically disqualify someone from going into politics. Present company aside, Tal. Your role isn't political, even though you're elected."

"Thanks for the distinction," Tal said. "I agree 100 percent."

"Political types use the term *public service* to ennoble it, but I don't buy that. Like the saying, 'To err is human. To blame it on someone else is politics.' The hot button for many people is abortion. Can you be skeptical about government, own guns, and still favor free choice when it comes to abortion? I do. Let the individual take responsibility." Jake paused and grinned shyly. "No one likes speechifying. I need to shut up."

"Not at all, not at all," Tal said. "We were hoping everyone could be at ease this evening. No need for this little group to hold back."

The succulent Pinot Noir continued to do its job. Inhibitions were disappearing. Jake took an appreciative sip and tilted his head back to let the deep burgundy liquid spill down the back of his tongue. He quietly inhaled across the roof of his mouth to oxygenate the cargo and slowly allowed it to drain down his throat, gently inhaling again to excite his taste buds and make them concentrate. He tasted black fruit surrounded by loamy earth recently moistened with rain. A tinge of metal—was it copper?— peeked through the earthiness and quickly morphed into the faintest hint of a cigar being smoked two rooms away. The alcohol hiding in the wine helped Jake relax almost instantly.

Tal continued, "Thanks for sharing your views. If you and our daughter are a couple, we want to know what makes you tick."

"I try to be totally straightforward," Jake said. "I'd like to think your daughter would agree."

"He's a straight arrow, for sure. He says what he'll do, and then does exactly that," Jess said.

Tal surveyed his daughter and Jake and then directed his comment to Ruth. "You can't ask for more than that, can you?"

She nodded. "No, you can't."

———◆———

A mile and a half from town, the Sasquatch leader raised an arm and the platoon stopped in unison. Silently, they sniffed the air and turned their heads to the left to listen for something. A feral pig sniffed and wiggled its way through the underbrush two hundred yards away. The creatures heard and smelled the pig's every movement. The leader made a low, quiet growl. Listening for another half minute, they heard the pig turn away, squeal a little, and start to run. The procession continued, slightly slower, as it approached the edge of Aurora.

———◆———

Jake twisted in his bow-legged antique chair and straightened his back before sharing more of his views with Jess's parents. He hoped his earnest confessions would erase the stigma Tal placed on his relationship with Jessica. "I don't like the mass media's saturation bombing. In the past, things moved at a stately pace. People got their information from each other or from a newspaper going into depth." He said news overkill in modern times was "a mile wide and an inch deep," part of the problem but not the solution. "People know about everything but actually know nothing. The news cycle makes everyone an expert. Everyone has an opinion about everything." Jake said Congress might as well be selected at random, like jury duty, rather than being elected in a sausage-making process determined by money. "Bottom line, we're exposed to too many words. If there's a problem: the sky is falling. We need earlids to match our eyelids. When's the last time you heard someone say, 'You know, I haven't really studied that subject in depth so I don't know enough to have an opinion'?"

"Hear, hear," Ruthie enthused.

Jake stopped and all was quiet.

Jessica spoke up. "Don't stop now, Jacob. You're on a roll."

"I'm talking too much. This fabulous wine is making me smarter."

"Jake, your views have merit," Tal said. "OK, I'll keep time. Two more minutes."

"We pass along our genetic faults and lose the goodness we were born with. Improvement happens at a glacier pace. We're flawed creatures, cursed to make the same mistakes over and over. Every life is an injustice and since we can't redeem ourselves, we hope there's a God to redeem us. There must be, or else we're nothing. For me, God is everything that exists in the universe, and yet he transcends it all—every atom and boson particle and quark and whatever else they discover day after tomorrow. It's called panentheism. William Blake said, 'Everything that lives is holy.' I think everything that *exists* is holy and is part of something we call *God*. Sometimes, if you really try, you can enter a room and sense the secret souls of everything—the plants and the chairs and the gyrating atomic particles that make up every single thing that exists."

"I can almost see the particles spinning in Eldo," Tal said, setting off a round of good-natured giggles.

"The big problems arrive when humans believe they have answers to questions that weren't asked," Jake continued. "All the suffering is created by us. We could eliminate it all, but we won't. At least not for a very long time. We can look straight into the eye of eternity, the unimaginable billions of years that came before us and the billions to come. But we understand nothing. Time doesn't end, but our time alive ends. There is no meaning to life, but there is life. That has to be enough. Plus the hope that there is something more."

Tal, Ruthie, and Jess pantomimed applause.

"Everything you said was thoughtful, Jake," Tal offered. "And it couldn't have been easy to be so open with us after our rather rocky history. I'm impressed. If you ever run for office, I hope it's not against me. For someone who doesn't care much for politics, you'd make one hell of a politician."

Ruthie smiled broadly. "Ditto on the thoughtful," she said, "but what politician could speak so honestly? Now, who's ready for some dinner?"

Ruth led them toward the dining room. Jess and her mother detoured through the kitchen to transport spit-roasted, free-range chickens, rosemary-roasted new potatoes, and grilled asparagus. Dessert was Ruthie's métier, and she would later outdo herself with maple crème brûlée. When she served it, she would remember to say, "Everything good is bad for you."

Jake turned to Tal as the group sat down. "It's your turn now," he said. "Time for you to hold forth about what's right and wrong with the world."

"All right. Well, there's a lot to like and even more to dislike," Tal began. "You and I are on the same page about a lot of things. Let's write a book." He paused. "But first let me tell you plainly that I overreacted when I charged you this morning—and especially when I let my own daughter get caught up in it. There was a body lying there that looked human-ish. I should have come up with something else. The hard part is finding a way to undo what's been done."

37

HEE-HAW'S 4—LET'S GO

It fell to a diminutive rooster of a man nicknamed Chigger to rally the troops in Hee-Haw's. James Albus "Chigger" Martin commanded the barroom's attention with his tale of a pacemaker murder. He said he'd read about it in the Seattle newspaper. In fact, he'd read it in the *National Enquirer*. Chigger had been divorced from his second wife for about six months, a messy drama involving a burial plot, a house trailer, a kid on meth, and several bad checks. He spent a great deal of time in the bar.

"This guy near got away with murder," Chigger intoned, clearing his throat for emphasis and sounding like he had a megaphone. "Turns out a pacemaker can have its timing turned up or down with this doohickey the heart doctors have. Supposed to be how they fine-tune it for the feller with the bad ticker. The doc sticks it on your chest and fiddles with it.

"So, this guy finds out about these adjusters, see, and gets to thinkin' about his rich father-in-law, who just got a pacemaker. He don't much like his wife's daddy, and the feelin' is mutual. Him and his wife's gonna get the money if the feller's dead 'cause there's not anybody else. He's tryin' to think how to get one of them adjusters. He's reading up on it. This ol' boy gets on the Internet, and hell if he don't find a complete set of plans on how they work. He manages a Radio Shack, so he knows a little about electronics. He up and builds one. Apparently, they are not all that complicated. You stick it on the pacemaker lump there on the chest and do what you want.

"Well, this guy done exactly that, it seems. Snuck up on his father-in-law at night while he's sound asleep and raced his heart fast as he could till he wasn't gonna wake up. Then he set the pacemaker back where it was and got home without anybody seein' him.

"The daughter found her daddy next day and called the police. Doctor came and said it looked like the feller's heart gave out. The autopsy came to the same conclusion. Case closed."

Chigger leaned against the bar and asked for another beer in a voice so soft it could barely be heard. He was quiet, but his silence was commanding. He took a sip from his fresh mug.

"OK, Chigger, you got us." The speaker was Einstein, the college boy. "You said he almost got away with murder. That means they must have caught him. You planning to tell us, or is this another Chigger tale?"

Chigger looked pleased. The silent routine had worked. "Sure enough, Einstein. I'll explain it to you. Then you tell me if I made it up. His wife got the money and didn't know a thing about what her husband done to her daddy.

Wasn't long till they were livin' it up pretty good. He bought him a new pickup and a boat. They bought computers and clothes and whatever else caught their fancy. Turns out, one dude on the local police kind of had his eye on them. He shot pool with the dead guy the ·same day he died, and the guy told him he was gettin' along great with his new pacemaker, never felt better. Made this policeman wonder about the whole deal. Well, like Ripley said, believe it or not, the cop walks into his living room one night right after his wife signed them up for cable. She's watching a medical program and the TV is explainin' how pacemakers work and it shows a doctor with one of them adjusters workin' on a heart patient. That local cop jumped straight up like his underwear had a battery and went back to work. Some detective from the highway patrol helped him. They looked into what the son-in-law had been buyin', and sure enough, he'd bought a bunch of electronic gizmos and whatnot for employee price at his Radio Shack. Ever' bit of it fit in with what they suspicioned. They found out where the adjusters are made and had a drawing sent to them, it bein' official police business. That guy had been buyin' just what you'd need to build one.

"The judge issued a search warrant, and they found switches and little batteries and wires he couldn't explain. They got some computer hotshot to look on his machine and—hell, did you boys know computers don't throw anything away? Well, they found pictures and diagrams of adjusters inside his computer. He couldn't explain that. They tried to get him to admit it, but he won't admit to nothin'. There's a trial startin' sometime soon—down in

Florida, I believe. The prosecutor won't talk much about it, but I allow they got him. Oughta put a pacemaker on him, and let somebody do a little adjustin'. A man that would kill his wife's daddy for the money—now that's a snake, boys."

Chigger paused for a breath. Einstein held up his index finger. "I guess it's possible, but given Chigger's rap sheet for tall tales, I'd give it about a six or seven of ten on the possibility scale. I believe they make pacemakers powered by lithium batteries that last five or ten years."

Chigger went on the attack. "Hell, Einstein, the murder was several years ago."

"But you said the trial was about to begin. And why would it be in the Seattle paper now if it happened years ago?"

"They just caught him a while back."

"But didn't you say the police started checking on the electronics he bought a little bit after the murder? That's what you said."

"Naw, I never said that." Chigger looked like he might be suffering a crisis of confidence, as if he'd recently gotten an adventuresome haircut. "Shoot, I don't know when it was. I wasn't plannin' on takin' a test, college boy."

"Well, true or not, it was a good story. I'll buy you a beer for the entertainment value. This was your best one since the Amish pimp, and right up there with the grand champion, your buddy who got drunk in his new suit and puked in his own lap, then went home and took a leak in his wife's underwear drawer. If I recall, the dog found the suit and chewed up the legs and crotch trying to eat the puke, right?"

"That's what happened," Chigger said.

"OK, then, order a beer on me. Fair enough?"

"You can buy me a case if you want to, Einstein. Coming from you, I especially appreciate it because you can't afford your own beer. But here's the other thing. I'm thinking it's about time to call up Oscar and go see the monster. It's gettin' dark outside."

Chigger's mention of Sasquatch sent a jolt through the beery congregation. The white-hot topic of what might or might not be lying in Oscar's funeral home had dominated the afternoon's bar talk, despite Chigger's tale. The initial conclusion suggested calling Tal O'Reilly to appear at the barroom to confirm or deny the Bigfoot scuttlebutt that had electrified Aurora. A few of the elbow benders thought calling Eldo might produce information, but most thought him too closemouthed and loyal to Tal to be useful.

In the end, Olympia beer and higher-octane fuels proved decisive to the revealed wisdom that the group should go to the funeral home and see for themselves. Mob mentality prevailed. Opinions grew more fiercely held, though often less intelligent. Not all joined the chorus. Several timid souls went home with comments along the lines of, "We need to stay out of it." Outside, the sky yielded to physics and transmuted to charcoal again. The beaten sun drooped, and the ashy dampness meshed with twilight. Exactly a dozen of Hee-Haw's finest eventually aligned themselves outside on Main Street. Despite the gloom of fading light, misty rain, and volcanic smoke, they advanced en masse toward the funeral home. Their conversation was unlike the needling bluster of the barroom. It was galvanized by an undercurrent of concern, if not fear.

Einstein called Oscar and suggested he hightail it to his place of business. Oscar finished his club sandwich and, in no hurry, walked his dog before adjourning to the funeral home. He was surprised at how nervous his usually calm Maltese behaved.

38

CONFRONTED—THEY'RE HERE

The dogs of Aurora were first to sense a change. The Sasquatch armada sailed into town from the north with utter stealth, their instincts for isolation on hold. A kinship of three brothers moved ahead of the other thirteen and acted as scouts, moving silently from tree to tree along the outer edges of town. The rest followed forty yards behind. The hiss of steady rain suffused with foggy volcanic smoke provided total cover, except to a bird dog's nose. A black Lab called Pete gurgled an affronted growl and barked with enthusiasm as he shot out of his driveway, ears down and neck fur up, toward the huge creatures walking the edges of his street. When the dog got close enough to make out the source of his olfactory panic, he clawed to a stop, backed up, and loosed a troubled howl. That kicked off a relay from other dogs within earshot, who bayed without knowing why. One of the Sasquatch tossed a small chunk of venison to Pete. He snatched it up and retreated with gratitude to his own yard.

The creature with red mud poultice on his shoulder was one of the scout brothers. He knew where he was going.

The others accepted his lead. The phalanx moved forward through the rain and smoke and ash. As they walked, they swung their long arms and looked warily from side to side. Several Aurorians peeked through mini blinds and curtains when they heard the dogs, but there was little to see except a smoggy dusk. Another ambitious dog was pacified with a scrap of raw meat as the unlikely pack moved through residential neighborhoods on a course that would take them directly past Ol' Vic on the way to Oscar's funeral home.

39

DAVE HUNTS THE STORY

Dave Hulett of *U.S. News & World Report* had caught a nonstop flight from DC to Portland scheduled to arrive at 5:30 p.m. The plane was on time. He got his rental car and a map with directions showing how to cross the Columbia River into Washington and hit the blue highways toward Aurora. He was on his way just after six as the spring light began to fade. The flight had been a smooth one until a half hour outside Portland, when the 737 was enveloped by rainstorms that were pelting the entire northwestern United States. Dave had hoped to see the fireworks from Mount St. Helens to the north and west as he approached Portland, but the wall of cloud and rain obscured any view outside the plane's windows. During the flight, he entertained himself with further tracking of the Sasquatch hubbub on the Internet, courtesy of the Boeing's satellite broadband connection. He also kept his laptop clacking by writing an imagined draft of the story he was chasing and by Internet chatting with his father and editor, Swann:

DAVE.   hey, pops. nonstop to portland, nearest city, and will
          drive north to aurora wash. net still buzzing about

bigfoot and volcano. likely a goose chase but one or other might make good copy.

SWANN go for it. potus knows and govt. is in. we don't have a cover this week so door is open if you make it fly. get local reaction, for sure, plus any law enforcement, etc. good luck.

DAVE. potus knows? how? guess they watch chat rooms too. no luck phoning sheriff but bet they did. hope all don't clam up before i get there.

DAVE. what do you think of my lede? (lol) . . . "Orthodox scientists and Bigfoot skeptics are eating crow since the recovery in tall-timber country of a Sasquatch corpse. The obscure southwest Washington town of Aurora has become Mecca to true believers in everything from flying saucers to dinosaurs in Loch Ness. Yes, there is the body of a previously unidentified creature coming to light, thanks in part to the Internet. But the rampant claims of kooks and shamans would make a carny barker blush."

SWANN. if you can prove even some of that, you'll have the cover. maybe more. suggest you keep low profile. see if you can talk to people without raising press flag. your mom and I are out to dinner tonight but will keep my cell handy. call as soon as you know anything.

DAVE. ok.

40

OL' VIC 4—LET'S HAVE A LOOK

Tal had made his comments about the day's events as furtive asides directed toward Jake and Jessica, but Ruth took note. She knew she was being left out of something important. As the evening progressed, the meaningful looks and obtuse comments snowballed. During a lull in the dinner conversation, she politely said to Tal, "I think maybe it's time you explained to me everything that's going on. Something obviously happened last night and this morning that you haven't shared."

"I've been asked not to talk about it."

"What do you mean, asked? Who asked you?" Ruth was trying to stay calm but was clearly nettled. "I'm part of this family, remember, and if something is going on involving us—"

"The president of the United States asked," Tal said. "But you're still right. I should have told you from the beginning. Let me explain." Tal proceeded to recount the events in full.

Ruthie was appalled. She let him know her displeasure. "Are you telling me because Jake shot something by accident, you're about to charge him with murder? And our own daughter with being an accessory? Talburt O'Reilly, have you lost your mind?"

Tal was sheepish. "Ruthie, I've tried to explain. We're about to become the center of the world. This creature looks so human I had to do something. Jess insisted on putting herself in the middle. What's the alternative?"

"I'll tell you the alternative," she said. "You march right down there after dinner to shred the paperwork and tell Eldo you got carried away and now you've changed your mind. Tell him to put a lid on it, which he'll do. There's your alternative. Then let the government people handle it when they get here."

There was silence and tension around the table. Tal looked from face to face as if waiting for a comment or hoping for teleportation to another dimension. No one spoke. He leaned back in his chair and ran a hand through his thinning hair. He pursed his lips. He could have been in a confession booth with his priest. "I suppose you're exactly right, Ruth. I guess I've made this worse than it needs to be." He paused. No one said a word. "I'll go to the courthouse after dinner."

The awkward moment lingered until Jess broke it. "OK, that's that," she said. "Pass the wine."

Jake started to reach for the wine and then stopped. He cocked an ear toward a bay window and said, "Does anyone else hear that? Why are the dogs howling?"

The four were silent again for a moment. "Could be the volcano has them spooked," Jess said. "Let's go outside and have a look."

41

MELEE—HUMANS ZERO

The events lasted only a few minutes, but every participant would remember it always. Not even the beasts would sleep peacefully for a while. The humans would never be the same. Modern *Homo sapiens* and upright bipedal hominids descended from a separate branch of evolution are not supposed to hang out with each other. The arc of impossible was disrupted. The fabric of routine was torn. Different species spun in the same vortex, compliments of the weather, a mountain, and Jake's unlucky gunshot.

Ruth saw them first, through the spindles of the side porch an instant before she was joined by Tal and Jess and Jake. She saw shadows silhouetted in the misty fog that quickly resolved themselves into living, moving creatures. Instinctively, she threw up her hands. She had an unmistakable view of a Sasquatch scout through the drizzle and ash. "My God," Ruthie said in a trembly voice two octaves higher than usual. "*Look look look look look.*" She dropped her wineglass down her front, spilling plummy juice on her white blouse.

The others looked where she pointed, though Tal took a nanosecond to register the loss of wine and an expensive goblet.

Jake scanned the scene across Ol' Vic's grassy moguls. He spotted the Sasquatch posse moving silently behind the scouts. He took charge, moving Ruth and Jessica behind him as he said, "Please listen carefully. I don't know if you can see them through the murk, but there are several. Move back into the house right now and hurry."

Tal put his arms around the women, and the party obliged.

Inside, Jake spoke with calm but urgent authority, as if he were prepared for dealing with crisis. "We need to turn on all the lights, especially outside. Can we do that?"

There were nods in the affirmative.

"Tal, do you have a gun in the house?"

"It's right here," he said, opening the drawer on a spindly hall table.

Jake said nothing but took the 9 mm Glock, shoved its clip into place, and cocked it. He moved toward the door.

"What are you doing? Jake, where are you going?" Jess asked.

He looked at her with a protective expression and hint of a smile. It conveyed love, concern, respect, and a trace of guilt. The creatures had come to Aurora. "Just to make sure no people are out there. If the neighbors see what I just saw, there could be problems. Please, Jess, stay here with your folks. Make sure the outside lights are on and the doors are locked." With that, Jake left through the stained glass front door, closing it securely behind himself.

Jess paused and looked over her shoulder at her parents. Ruth and Tal were flipping on every light switch they could find. "Lock up behind me," Jess said as she slipped out the same door thirty seconds behind Jake.

"Wait a minute—" Tal objected as Jess closed the door and disappeared.

Was it was preordained that men and Sasquatch would intersect? Main Street—where Hee-Haw's was situated and where the less-than-salubrious human contingent had gathered and marched toward Oscar's—crossed Locust Street about a block from Ol' Vic and near the funeral home. There was a green sign noting the two street names and a thick asphalt road crossing that was melty on hot summer days. The curb was broken in two places. An army truck had swerved during a training maneuver in 1943 and cracked off a chunk. The other flaw was where Dan Clopten smacked the curb in 1964 on a Flexible Flyer snow sled being towed by Hogic Samsel driving his dad's new Plymouth. The ordinary street intersection would become a place of legend for generations of Aurorians to come.

Hee-Haw led the human pack. When his customers began their march up Main, he yelled that he'd be back in a bit to the old man staying behind to watch the register. Albert immediately went to the front with Chigger, his ample beer belly decorated with cheeseburger grease, pointing the way. As the quorum approached Main and Locust, the rain and smoky ash had thinned slightly, allowing a bit of visibility. Still, considering the damp fog and persistent steam from Loowit, it was a bit like stepping out of a long hot shower and squinting at your useless vanity mirror. A city streetlight with one gloomy bulb hung twenty-five feet up a pole on the corner. Young Billy Lasswell and Chuck Wooten hid in the bushes of an adjacent yard. They had staked out Hee-Haw's back door an hour earlier and successfully completed some expert eavesdropping.

The Sasquatch arrived first. Their preternatural senses assured they knew something was coming well before the men entered the intersection. The sixteen beasts hid themselves behind the oaks lining Main and listened and watched as the damp procession of men marched noisily up the street. The beasts had glowing eyes, like many nocturnal predators, that gave them night vision as keen as infrared goggles. Their eyes swiveled like those of chameleons as they took note of every detail. The beery marchers heard and saw nothing unusual. As the humans crossed over Locust, the Sasquatch leader took action. He stepped from behind a tree into the street in front of the dozen men. He raised his massive arms with doubled fists over his head and loosed, from his eight-foot-tall body, a bellowing howl that curdled the blood of everyone who heard it, including Jake, a half block away and closing fast. The other Sasquatch quickly followed the leader's howl with their own as they shucked their cloak of mystery and stepped from their hiding places to posture aggressively. Pandemonium ensued. The beasts' deep yowling produced an aggregate clamor and roar like a passing tornado. The result was an outcry from Hee-Haw's posse like soldiers caught in an ambush. Cursing and shouting and entreaties to heaven were yelled as the frightened men sought escape. There was confusion and hubbub, but it wasn't a contest. Sasquatch, twelve; humans, zero.

The male Bigfoot leader showed little sign of his gunshot flesh wound. He bellowed again and in a split second was directly in front of Chigger and Hee-Haw. The other creatures took his cue and moved to confront the other men.

"Oh, God, Mother Swearingen!" Hee-Haw shouted.

Chigger couldn't make a sound. He raised an arm over his face in a defensive gesture.

The Bigfoot emitted a low growl and shoved Chigger backward with a thump to his chest. It was like being hit with a cannonball. Chigger was airborne for an instant and then landed in a heap and slid to the curb. His clothes were disheveled and his knees skinned. He scrambled to his feet and raced down the sidewalk toward the tavern, squealing a high-pitched "*Shiiiiiit!*" as he ran.

The others fared no better. With a sweep of his wounded arm, the Sasquatch leader dispatched Hee-Haw into a tumble. He rolled down the street like a snowboarder gone wrong. Hee-Haw leaped up and tried to run but tripped on an uneven chunk of asphalt and fell again, pulling his hamstring. His retreat featured a noticeable limp.

Edgar Lasswell reacted to the bellowing beasts by bellowing back in fear, as one might yell at a strange dog's approach. "Aaaarrr!" he growled in his best basso profundo, simultaneously backstepping in the direction from which he'd come. A Sasquatch approached Edgar closely, raised up to his full height, and then bent down in Edgar's face. The creature bared his teeth and snapped them twice. No additional convincing was necessary. Untouched, Edgar hightailed it with Chigger and Hee-Haw.

Beverly Porter, always compensating for his girlish name, attempted machismo. He had a flash of bravado and yelled, "Don't run! Don't run!" to his comrades. "Don't run from these sumbitches!" He tried to posture aggressively, but his feet had other ideas and danced backward. Reading Beverly's body language and vocal cues, a Sasquatch took two strides forward and used his leg like a sling blade. Beverly went down like a rag doll, his arms and legs windmilling. It was a move the beasts used on spooked deer. Beverly came up with ripped pants and a raw rump. The macho was gone. His body surged with adrenaline, and he nearly knocked down Doug the Dead Dog Dude as he turned tail and ran. His ripped pants exposed Beverly's white boxers as he fled, causing the Sasquatch to picture a white-tailed buck amid the melee.

T-Bone was farther back in the posse and set sail the instant he heard the beastly roar. No one noticed how quickly he moved for a big man.

Einstein was near the back of the pack with the college buddy he'd brought from the bar. He imagined himself a detached observer from the start, telling his pal, "I've got to see how this turns out. There won't be any Sasquatch to see." The first howl hadn't died when Einstein and his friend were gone in a blaze of youthful running speed. They saw nothing other than dark shapes. They heard the grunts and scuffles as they fled. They were the first back to Hee-Haw's. By next evening, however, both would describe the scene in intricate detail to their Sunday-night dates. The girls would meet in the bathroom and decide it was obvious the boys had fabricated the tale.

LR and Cotton walked as a team from the bar to the intersection, chatting away at each other. They were just behind Hee-Haw and Chigger. It was LR who didn't survive. When he saw the Sasquatch mob emerge from the trees, his heart raced, and he turned fish-belly white as he crumpled to the street. His grimace exposed his troubled teeth, which he always tried to hide. Cotton kept his cool and helped LR back to his feet and away from the confrontation, but he had to support him as they stumbled away. LR's left ventricle was so clogged that it didn't take much to send his heart over the edge. With Cotton holding him up, a gasping LR made it back to Hee-Haw's front door before passing out. An ambulance was called to whisk LR to the hospital.

Jake arrived only seconds after the Sasquatch leader tossed Hee-Haw and Chigger aside. Jess followed half a block behind. Though visibility had slightly improved, there was still such confusion in the fog and mist and ash that it was impossible to see what was happening. Jake raised the Glock and crouched on the sidewalk in a two-handed, police-style shooting pose. He saw Chigger and Hee-Haw running away. The Sasquatch leader he wounded the day before came into view down the gun barrel. Man and beast froze, each recognizing the other from twenty feet away.

The Sasquatch bared his teeth and issued a deep gurgle.

Jake slipped his finger inside the trigger guard.

Jessica ran into the picture. She saw the animal, and pure fear suffused her body. Her legs went to jelly, like those of a newborn gazelle. She promptly tripped on the dark curb, stumbled into the street, and fell at the Sasquatch's feet.

The creature lowered his best arm in a split second and raised Jessica up in front of him, a huge arm under her chin. Her eyes were wild, but she made no sound. Her arms reached out toward Jake, and her trembling hands opened and closed frantically. She wanted to make a sound, to scream bloody murder, to say, "I love you." But nothing came out. She couldn't breathe. The Sasquatch's thick arm was cutting off her air supply. She gasped again and again.

Jake didn't shout or panic. In a clear and determined voice, he said, "Put her down." He pointed toward the ground with the hand not holding the gun. He said it louder. "*Put her down!*" He motioned downward again while moving closer.

Now Jake stood just ten feet away. He pointed the pistol at the creature's huge head, which towered above Jessica's. It was a clear enough shot to take if he chose to take it, but at ten feet, Jake could also see into the creature's eyes well enough to recognize its hurt and near humanity. He didn't pull the trigger. He looked into the Sasquatch's face and knelt down. He moved himself forward on his knees until he was at the beast's feet in a gesture that clearly conveyed *hurt me, but don't hurt her*. He put the pistol on the ground.

He looked up at the huge creature and pleaded, "Put her down." Again he motioned downward. He glanced to locate the pistol in case he had no choice but to grab it and fire.

The Sasquatch released Jessica a moment before she would have passed out. She gulped air and pulled herself unsteadily toward the curb.

The creature looked at Jake and pointed a finger the size of a pepper mill down the street toward Ol' Vic. He poked the top of Jake's head with the finger, a glancing blow clearly intended not to injure. Jake's skull vibrated, and his neck snapped backward. The Sasquatch turned and vanished into the mist, moving with its comrades toward the funeral home.

42

OSCAR'S 4—THE CORPSE IS GONE

The deed was done quickly and efficiently. By sniffing the air, the male leader easily located the tree where he'd scooped up Billy Lasswell the night before. Across the street was the funeral home's back door. The lock was no obstacle; it yielded with a powerful tug. The padlock on the cold room required two blows of increasing force from an arm and fist the equal of a sledgehammer. The lone night-light was enough for creatures whose night vision exceeded an owl's. Two males who entered with the wounded leader picked up the corpse and carried her outside. They left her covered in Oscar's rubber sheet, tucking it carefully around her, which trapped Tal's videotape inside. The Sasquatch moved with determination in the direction from which they came.

As the creatures departed, Oscar was fumbling with his keys at the front door. He'd tried to call Tal when the bar crowd demanded he come to his business, but got no answer. He had to deal with them alone. "So where are all of Hee-Haw's boys?" he said to himself as he unlocked the door. "Surprised they're not here yet."

He planned to tell them he didn't have a key to the cold room padlock and they'd have to find Tal. Oscar flipped on the lights and went straight to the rear. He saw the cold room door standing open with a broken lock and the empty gurney inside. "What in the name of . . . Why in the Sam Hill couldn't the boys wait until I got here?" he asked the empty room.

He hurried to the back door and looked into the gloom but saw nothing. He looked down at his floor and saw muddy swirls on the vinyl. Had he looked more carefully, he might have articulated huge footprints, but Oscar was a meticulous man, and what he saw was a mess. There were streaks and whorls of slimy, ashy mud, as if his tiles were a modernist painting. He shook his head, opened a closet, and extracted cleaning supplies. He would wipe everything down and call Tal. The bar crowd was out of control, he thought, and now they had the Sasquatch body.

The creatures didn't leave town without incident. A fearless Rottweiler who lived three blocks away was agitated—first by the other dogs baying and then by the Sasquatch howls and unknown smell wafting through the air. It was nature. Though he'd never escaped before, Bodo leaped at his wire fence and caught his claws halfway up, allowing him to heave and scrabble his way free. He was patrolling the ashy fog in an excited state when he happened on the rear echelon of the departing Sasquatch. He charged. The thick hair behind his head stood high, as did his tail. A smaller Sasquatch, one of two teenagers in the group, smelled and heard the attack and turned to receive it. Bodo sent his one hundred thirty pounds through the air at the beast, teeth bared. The Sasquatch youth closed his great fist and swung his arm like a tennis backhand, striking the dog on the neck and chest. Bodo issued a single, muted yelp and fell to the ground as limp as earlobes. The dog's feet twitched. He was unconscious for two minutes. The Rottweiler recovered, but his docile nature thereafter was a surprise to his owner.

The events of Saturday night in Aurora didn't go unnoticed by residents along the way, but try as they might, conditions prevented anyone from seeing anything with clarity. Noses pressed against windows, doors creaked open, and a tentative step or two was taken onto a porch. The hellish mix of ash and rain and steam and fog wafting through town was like a curtain. No cars were in sight. The Sasquatch funeral cortege continued out of town. The creatures were soon again enveloped by the giant trees and dense vegetation. Since they shed virtually none of their hair, outsized and indistinct muddy footprints were the only things left behind. Ever the collusionist, El Niño, the baby, turned the drizzle into a persistent rain, and its machine-gun battering caused nearby puddles to swirl and foam. The water washed away all evidence that Aurora had been invaded.

43

HEE-HAW'S 5—EINSTEIN GETS IT

As LR was taken by ambulance to the hospital, the waterlogged posse reconvened at the bar. One of the men stood by the front door and kept a lookout up and down Main Street. The earlier ebullience had vanished. Hurried phone calls were made warning family and friends to stay inside. Hee-Haw laid his shotgun on the bar and announced free beer. The frightened crew would have been abstemious, but free beer made them drink like skinny dogs and whisper to each other. Various opinions, all of them wrong, tried to explain what had happened and why the creatures had suddenly lost their reclusiveness.

The female college professor nicknamed Spoon had been well to the rear of the posse but still had heard some of the fracas. She tried to change the mood. "Well, gentlemen, one thing's for sure. That's not something you see every day. Now we've got something to talk about besides the terrorists."

"I hope LR is all right," said Ed Lasswell. "He didn't look so good. You know, I told y'all Billy wouldn't lie about this Bigfoot deal. He damn sure didn't."

Beverly Porter fussed with his ripped pants and tried to hide his backside from the others.

Oscar Marsh walked into the room. It was clear from his expression that he hadn't come to chat.

"Hey, Oscar, where have you been?" asked Hee-Haw. "Come have a free beer."

"I've been cleaning up the nasty mess you idiots made in my funeral home," Oscar said. "Who's paying for the broken locks and the door and my rubber sheet? And what have you done with that corpse? Tal O'Reilly's gonna be fit to be tied."

The bar was quiet. All eyes were on Oscar as the crew tried to interpret his statement. Oscar looked around, expecting to see the Sasquatch body stretched out on the floor. "Well?"

Einstein got it. "Hell's bells," he said. "There really was a Bigfoot corpse, and they came to take it back. Sit down, Oscar. This will blow your mind."

44

OL' VIC 5—SURVIVORS

Jake and Jess pounded on Ol' Vic's front door and yelled for Marie and Tal to let them back in. Jake handed the pistol to Tal, who removed the clip and put it back into the hall table.

Tal and Ruthie understood clearly that something bad had happened.

Jess reached from under Jake's protective arm and hugged her mother, then slid back close to him. He pulled her tight and kissed her softly on the cheek in front of her parents. He wiped rainwater off her face and his own. She took a deep breath, and a small shudder escaped. Both tried to slow their breathing.

Jake looked directly at Tal, who silently mouthed, *What happened?*

"We ran straight into several of those creatures near the funeral home," Jake said quietly. "People from Hee-Haw's were there. The one I wounded in the shoulder was there, and Jess and I got a little too close."

"I'm so sorry," Jessica interrupted. "You asked me to stay here, but I couldn't."

"It's OK. Really, it's OK," Jake tried to soothe her. "We're fine now. Don't worry about it. Maybe I shouldn't have gone outside either. I was afraid there might be kids out there, or neighbors who heard something. It's my responsibility. I have an idea why they came into town."

Jake explained to Tal and Ruthie what happened and how the bar posse retreated, and although he couldn't see very well, he thought they all got away. He described the standoff with the Sasquatch. He said something told him to lay down the gun rather than fire it. "There was intelligence in his eyes when I got close enough to see him," Jake said. "They almost glowed in the dark. I was asking and motioning for him to put Jess down. I know he didn't understand the words, but I think he understood my gesture. As soon as I put the weapon down, he let Jess go. Then he pointed for us to go back where we came from, and we thought that was a good idea."

"Lord have mercy," Tal said. "I didn't believe they existed at all, and now we not only have a corpse, we have a whole herd. Thank God both of you are all right. What made them come marching into town? I wonder."

"I think they went to Oscar's," Jake said. "Tal, I think they came to get the body."

Tal raised his eyebrows and nodded slowly. "Sure," he said. "If they're as smart as you think, that makes perfect sense. Jake, do you think we'd be safe in a car? We could drive to Oscar's and see what's happening."

"I don't think they're trying to hurt anybody," Jake said. "They had a perfect chance to do that if they wanted. We should be fine inside a car. At worst, we could just drive away. Jess, why don't you and your mom stay here with the doors locked."

"No way," Ruth said. "We're going. We all go together."

In sixty seconds, the four were in Tal's SUV, backing out of the garage. They drove very slowly to Oscar's without headlights, which in any case were useless in the rain and steam. They saw the back door twisted on its hinges and the night-light illuminating the open door to the cold room. Oscar had already cleaned up and gone.

"You were right, Jake," Tal said. "They came for the corpse, and now they're gone. We won't see them again."

"There's no sign of them up or down the street," Jake said, "at least as far as I can see. I'll bet they're out of town by now."

"God in heaven," Ruth said. "What next?"

"I'd suggest we drive by Hee-Haw's and make sure the boys and girls are all right," Jake said. "I don't know about anyone else, but by then I'll be ready to call it a night. OK with you, Jess?"

"Way OK by me."

45

PARANORMAL GROUP

The PNG's mission statement stressed keeping a low profile and reporting directly to the White House. Every asset of the government of the United States of America was at their disposal, which meant that Major Lucas Cooper had a powerful, if covert, job. He commanded the PNG, so he was responsible for scrambling the Core Corps, a group of twenty-four elite PNG soldiers, when he got the code-red call. The heart of the CC spent much of that Saturday in May on an air force jet bound for the airport near Seattle, nicknamed Sea-Tac. They disembarked at a private hangar well away from the main terminal and entered four black GMC Denali SUVs for the drive south to Aurora.

The men were hyperaware of their surroundings and moved with purpose and economy. Major Cooper knew that Portland International Airport was closer to his target than Sea-Tac, but he needed to go where secure facilities were prearranged and prying eyes unlikely. The men wore cotton chinos and loose camp shirts in random colors. They could have been heading to a class reunion except for steel-toed boots under the creased cuffs of their khakis, the tiny wire running from the neck of their shirts to what looked like a hearing aid, and the black microphone the size of a dime clipped on their collars. Not to mention that each shirt also covered a Browning .38.

Cooper and his men knew Mount St. Helens had a case of indigestion and was belching smoke and ash from her cauldron toward their coordinates. They'd been briefed repeatedly on their flight from Fort Meade in Maryland. They didn't know what they would encounter in Aurora, but like all military men, they knew it wouldn't go according to plan. Had they arrived in time to confront the squadron of Sasquatch, the result might have been chaos for man and beast alike. They did not.

The creatures were long gone when the Denalis rolled down Main Street. However, what the PNG corps wasn't prepared for was Hee-Haw's. The soldiers rolled up and down the barren and ashy streets for half an hour but saw nothing unusual. Cooper noted the neon donkey and the gathering within. After removing their communication wires, he took three men inside to get their ears full. After an hour, the major gave an imperceptible signal, and the four retreated to their vehicles, rewired, and drove to the edge of town. The call to the White House Situation Room was connected immediately. It was unlike any such call before.

MAJOR COOPER. PNG here. Scramble, please. I need Stanton Buckley.

AIDE. Roger. Call encrypted. . . . I'll put Buckley on.

BUCKLEY. Stan here. What've you got, Luke?

COOPER.   I'm not sure. This operation is pretty loose. We're here with boots on the ground, but we can't see a damn thing. Between the ash from St. Helens and the drizzle and fog, this place is rolled up tight. All I've got is a handful of bar stories right now.

BUCKLEY.   You're in a bar? How is that supposed to keep you below the radar?

COOPER.   Just myself and three others went into the bar. There was no other way to learn anything. We drove around, but there was nothing to see. Our cover made us into college accreditors getting ready to check out the local juco. We heard some interesting stories.

BUCKLEY.   I get the picture. Tell me about it.

COOPER.   Sir, there are several people here who claim they've seen a large group of Sasquatch— maybe twenty or thirty—on the streets of Aurora. They say there was a confrontation with these creatures and one of their buddies was taken to the hospital, probably with a heart attack. No other injuries to report. They say a local guy shot and killed a female Sasquatch yesterday, and the body was in the local funeral parlor. And these Sasquatch supposedly came into town and removed the body. Their stories are remarkably consistent even though they're all drinking. I'd have to say they're credible.

But as far as I know from our recon and the firsthand accounts, there isn't a shred of physical evidence for corroboration. The rain and ash are taking care of any new footprints or other trail evidence, and the guy who owns the funeral home thought his buddies broke in, so he cleaned up his floors and walls with commercial cleaners. I doubt there's anything there.

BUCKLEY.   Major, are you telling me you've got credible witnesses but no evidence? We've had credible Sasquatch stories for decades, but no hard evidence. We launched your group because we had sparks flying about a Sasquatch body. Is there a body or not?

COOPER.   There might have been, but apparently it's gone. That's what these folks are telling me. I've got an undertaker named Oscar who says there was a Sasquatch corpse in his funeral home until an hour or two ago. He says they made a videotape of it this morning. He and the others say a gang of these creatures marched right in through the murk and took the body away.

BUCKLEY.   A video? Did you say there's a video?

COOPER.   *Was* a video. The undertaker says he and the local sheriff and the prosecuting attorney, who seems to be the go-to guy around here, made a video of the Sasquatch corpse this morning. But now it's gone. Oscar says he was cleaning up because he thought his buddies had the body and the video. But supposedly the bar crowd ran into the Sasquatch and were run off before they got to the funeral home. Wild story, huh? Several of them are pretty wasted. No one saw much or can prove anything, but they claim the body and video are gone.

BUCKLEY. You're saying there's absolutely no physical evidence? No footprints, no hair, no blood?

COOPER. Not as far as we can tell. We haven't combed the town or the mortuary yet, but there's this unholy fog and rain mixed with smoke and volcanic ash. It's hard for me to see how there could be anything to find. But you do have a bunch of eyewitnesses.

BUCKLEY. Major, I suppose you've heard of mass hysteria?

COOPER. Sure.

BUCKLEY. Sit tight. Talk to no one. Keep your cover. We're going to make a quick call here. Let me talk to POTUS, and I'll get right back with you. Got it?

COOPER. Yes, sir. Absolutely.

46

MOTHER CAVE—A FUNERAL

Unwelcoming topography forced the creatures to zigzag through the tall trees, but with their long, tireless gaits, they reached the cave in slightly more than two hours. They were silent as they walked and took turns carrying the body wrapped in its rubber sheet with the video. Despite their unholy size, they made only a faint shuffling sound, passing efficiently and quickly through the forest. They were careful where they walked. A Sasquatch in full stride seemed to grasp the ground with its huge feet and pull the earth backward.

The cave was situated three thousand feet above and fifteen miles from Aurora. It might as well have been on a different continent. The creatures, however, knew where they were, where they'd been, and where they were going. They shared an infallible sense of dead reckoning and sensitivity for magnetic north of many wild animals. Once inside the cave, they easily scaled the near-vertical wall that protected them from casual discovery, a wall that humans would have needed lamps and pitons and hammers and clips and ropes and spiked shoes to surmount. But humans were unlikely to discover the wall in the first place. The Sasquatch handed up the body with considerable effort, then moved again as a group through the black hole of darkness to a rocky walkway. They vocalized like bats to find their way, issuing guttural grunts that echoed off the cave walls. Deeper and deeper the pallbearers proceeded until the darkness gave way to a faint fire glow. Others of their kind—young, old, or female— waited around the fire. Smoked venison and juniper-rubbed wapatoo awaited the returning heroes. The videocassette and mortuary sheet went into the fire and were consumed. They laid the body down and ate ravenously, then used their hands to catch water that seeped in trickles down the walls. They lapped it from their palms like African omnivores over a Serengeti puddle.

The Sasquatch leader rubbed more clay poultice onto his injured shoulder. He made a low rumble that translated into a signal. Two females picked up the corpse and entered an opening to the rear of the huge cavern room where the fire's flicker cast moving shadows on the wet walls. Four of the others picked up burning sticks to use as torches. The entire group entered the passageway. The torches illuminated a series of openings, and the group proceeded through one of them and down a rocky ramp to another huge room that could have contained a football field. When the body carriers and torchbearers entered ahead of the others, the light revealed thousands of Sasquatch skeletons laid out in rows against the walls. It looked as if human giants had been carefully lying down and dying for eons. The body was expertly placed in a section among the more recently deceased, as evidenced by varying stages of decomposition. The beasts ignored the malodorous stench.

The bereaved male moved forward and knelt by his mate's body. He ran his hand through his untonsured hair and then through her shorn locks as if to straighten them. He lowered his head.

The others made soft humming noises clearly intended to express condolence. The sound was rhythmic, almost musical.

The torches illuminated the stone walls of the mausoleum and revealed striations of earthy color, along with grooves and niches and spirals. Along the walls in every direction were decorations made with crude paint composed of chopped-up plant material mixed with animal fat. There were stick figures of running deer along with unrecognizable animals, intricate geometric patterns, the moon in various phases alongside the sun, and hundreds of rudimentary faces.

The huge male again ignored his injured shoulder and picked up a dimpled flat rock that held three colors in its depressions. He solemnly dipped a thick finger into the gelatinous liquid and began to form the face of his partner on the wall. The torches were held closer so he could see, and the mourners could watch with approval.

47

MORNING—LR IS DEAD

A new front of powerful rain would return by late afternoon and gurgle in Aurora's gutters, but Sunday morning broke bright and clear. The air was free of Loowit's swirling ash thanks to an overnight wind shift. Plenty of sweeping up remained. The mountain still had a notable case of reflux and burped a steady cloud of gas and steam from her belly. Minor tremors shook her flanks five times an hour, on average. The white cloud above her rose thousands of feet straight up and then bent suddenly to the north and east. For the first time in history, Hee-Haw's was in violation of state liquor laws. The tavern was open on Sunday morning by popular demand. The owner had called Eldo about nine.

"Morning, Eldo. Not sure what to do about it, but I've got a bunch of regulars over here wanting me to open up today. I came in to clean a little and tap new kegs, and these boys are after me to open the doors. What do you think?"

"I drove by a while ago and saw them outside," Eldo said. "I kind of expected you to call. I'm told several of them went back up to Main and Locust this morning but didn't

239

find a thing. Not even a footprint. Apparently, there are folks hearing the story who don't believe it. They think your crowd is making it all up for a gag. I drove there myself. There's nothing to see unless you notice all the birds. The trees are full of birds, just sitting there, all different kinds. I don't know what to make of that. Maybe there's a smell we can't detect. I guess you've heard about LR?"

"Not a word. That's why some of the boys are outside. They're wanting to know about him. He gonna be all right?"

"Afraid not. He didn't make it."

"What? Are you saying LR is dead?"

"He died early this morning, Al. I'm sorry. The hospital said he had a bad heart to start with."

"Well, Jesus, Mary, and Joseph, Eldo. I had no idea. Damn. Double damn. Do any of the guys outside know?"

"I don't think so. I just got the call."

"Good Lord. This is gonna take some getting used to. Ol' LR could cuss the gate off its hinges, and he lied so much his wife had to call the dog, but every man Jack of us liked the son of a gun."

"I know. I liked him too. But he never had a wife."

"Yes, Eldo. I know. Just a figure of speech. Well, doesn't this just take the cake. Things weren't weird enough already, and now LR is dead. Will you look the other way if I let them in? I need to tell them, one way or the other. They just want to jaw about the whole experience."

"Brother Swearingen, you didn't hear me say this, but do what you will. If the preachers get after you, you're on your own. Just don't let them get rowdy. And maybe close back down around lunchtime. Now here's another thing. I've got two journalists here at the courthouse who came at two this morning and slept in their car. They want me to tell them what's going on. I'm not telling them anything. But that's not the half of it. Al, one of them is from Japan and the other from India. They say they've been traveling for God knows how long to get here, and they seem to know quite a bit already. I don't know how. I'll send them your way. It's a free country. If the boys and girls at your place don't confuse them, no one can. OK by you?"

"Sure, Eldo. I'm opening the door right now. But if journalists are here, that has to mean the whole world knows, doesn't it? Come by and give us a little help, if you can."

48

HEE-HAW'S 6—DIGGING FOR THE STORY

The exotic journalists didn't want to seem inept when their linguistic skills were stretched beyond the comfort zone, especially Kenzo. He and Ashok listened carefully to the bar stories and nodded in amazement. Factoring in the level of colloquialisms and questionable diction, they understood about half the words spewing from the raffish crew, but the unfolding story was clear enough. The eyewitnesses stepped forward without hesitation and told it all from their particular point of view. Most added a dab of color, others outright exaggeration. Kenzo and Ashok were all business. They asked questions; they took notes. They got plenty to work with. Dave Hulett had also arrived, discovered the tavern, and taken an inconspicuous barstool. He tried to listen without identifying himself, but Hee-Haw saw him sneaking notes as the tales swirled about. He asked Dave if he was also a journalist, like Kenzo and Ashok. Dave admitted he was and decided to play his Washington card.

"Actually, I'm with *U.S. News & World Report*," he said a little too smugly. "We're only online now, but we also do special issues about big events. So I'm just like you folks—from Washington—just the one on the other side of the country." Dave smiled expectantly, but his little joke fell flat. "This is quite a story unfolding around here. I hope you don't mind me listening in."

"Be my guest," Hee-Haw offered. "But good luck making any sense out of this bunch." He gestured at the gathering with a sweep of his arm. "Most of them are ugly as homemade soap, and if their lips are moving, they're lying."

Dave inserted himself into the scene quickly, asking questions and jotting answers with a cavalier expression. "So I guess you guys are saying these things are pretty smart," he asked the company in general.

A house painter nicknamed Mike, because he claimed to paint houses like Michelangelo, answered, "Smart? Hell, you could see how smart they were. More like humans than anything. They were in town on a mission, and they stuck to it. They could have torn us up, but they didn't."

"He's got a point," Einstein said. "None of us knew what was happening until it was over. But the creatures knew what they were doing. They were like an army platoon, except for the growling. As I look back on it, they didn't want to hurt us, but they made us hurt ourselves."

"You know why we call him Einstein?" asked T-Bone, looking at the three journalists.

Dave and Kenzo and Ashok waited.

"Because he's got a brain just like Einstein's. Dead since 1955." T-Bone had used the line before, but it still produced a collective smirk.

Encouraged by Dave Hulett's momentary attention, Mike launched into his standard riff for a new listener. He explained to Dave how his grandfather had owned the building they were in and operated a grocery store there during the Great Depression. He'd offered a special promotion just before Thanksgiving and Christmas. Mike declared, "A day or two before the holiday, my daddy used to tell me, Grandpa would climb up on top of the building with a cageful of clipped chickens and turkeys. A helluva crowd would gather down below. He'd throw those birds off the top of the building, and whoever could catch one had their holiday dinner for free. Their wings still worked a little, so they'd flutter down and take off. Some of them made it two or three blocks, and people would run over each other to get a bird. Can you imagine that scene? My daddy worked for Grandpa when he was a boy of ten or twelve. Said he got paid two dollars for working six in the morning till six at night."

"He's telling the truth because my father caught one of those birds." The speaker was Beverly Porter. "It didn't turn out very well, though. My dad and his brother heard how you can dress out a turkey by hanging it upside down and then cutting its throat. The feathers are supposed to pull right off in handfuls after it bleeds out. So they took the bird home and hung it by its feet with some old twine they found. They did it in the bathroom, and had a bucket to catch the blood. But when they cut that turkey's throat, the damned thing went wild. It fought and scrabbled so hard it broke the twine and fluttered and flopped all over that little bathroom. It spewed blood and guts everywhere. Dad said the bathroom looked like it had been painted red, and it took him and his brother four hours to clean it up."

The bar clock ticked relentlessly forward. Hee-Haw began clearing the illegal customers out about noon. They all went home feeling unsettled, and for the next few days their usual banter was somewhat stunted. They hadn't yet arrived at a standardized version of the recent events in Aurora. In the days and weeks and months and years to come, the gaps between versions would only widen.

49

HOME SWEET HOME 2—SADNESS

Jacob wept. He awoke from a deep nap Sunday afternoon gasping for breath with tears in his eyes, the result of a wrenching dream featuring his deceased parents as teenagers. It was a strong, clear dream, the kind that seems like reality. He'd seen them in the bloom of youth walking the hallways of their Missouri high school holding hands.

They were genuine high school sweethearts, never dating anyone else and spending all their free time together. They married a week after graduation. In the dream, they were talking about having children one day. They were talking about Jake and his older sister. Seeing them so young and full of life and hope had been deeply unsettling to Jake when he awoke. Their life together hadn't been the one they'd imagined. Like most relationships, theirs had its share of heartache. Living together in marriage was harder than strolling the high school hallways. Jake's sister wasn't born until they were well past thirty. Jake was three years later. They divorced in their sixties after more than forty years together. They died four months apart in their early seventies. Neither had ever found another partner or moved from their hometown.

Jake's agitated sleep had also conjured Bigfoot monsters. The dark and mysterious creatures had boiled in and out of his thoughts since the shot was fired two days before. Now they had invaded his sleep. After he was fully awake, Jake wondered whether he would ever be able to make them go away. He noticed with gratitude, however, that his ears had stopped ringing. As he thought back on it, he realized the tinnitus, which had started with his gunshot, had stopped the previous night when the Sasquatch thumped his head.

Jess was puttering in the kitchen from the sound of things. She was humming to herself. She was a fabulous and creative cook, taking joy in the process of putting together interesting ingredients to make memorable meals. They would eat well later that evening. Arctic char tartare over daikon radish spears with trout caviar; baby asparagus salad with lemongrass and cauliflower snow; grilled hanger steak with homemade potato chips and blue cheese sauce. Their conversation over dinner would include the obvious—volcanoes and ancient beasts—but would also encompass a range of topics worthy of Jess's meal: how steel boats can float, earthquakes and continental drift, the proper way to clip toenails, and the migration patterns of monarch butterflies. Jake would explain that he had seen a cable TV documentary on butterfly migration. He would describe it in detail. Then Jess would say, "That tells me everything I should know except one thing—why?"

Jake would compliment her over and over on the meal and ask why she'd gone to such effort, though he would know her answer in advance.

"We will never again be allowed to live this wonderful day," she would say.

Jake went into the bathroom to relieve himself. As he stared at the wall, the phrase *American yeti* rolled through his head. He thought about how things acquired their names. He preferred names that made common sense. Bumblebee Pass, Quartz Creek, the Sawtooth Range—these made sense, he thought, along with good old Bigfoot. But American yeti? Why was Bigfoot sometimes called the American yeti? The yeti was the Abominable Snowman claimed to roam in the Himalayas of Asia. He thought that Abominable Snowman was a fine, commonsense name, one that fit the locale.

Jake assessed himself in the bathroom mirror and saw he needed a shave and his hair was in rebellion. He flooded his head with water and gave the hair a quick brushing. He noticed a couple of loose hairs stuck near the sink's drain. He stared at the hairs for a moment and then sucked in his breath and said, "Oh my."

Jake strode quietly but purposefully out the back door to the barn. He handed Split Log an apple from a bushel of culls near the door, then opened the saddlebags hanging on the stall railing. Jake took out the plastic Ziploc he'd forgotten about and held it up to the light of the barn door. He could clearly see the wad of bloody hair, tissue, and bone fragments he'd scraped from under the dead Sasquatch before loading her on his makeshift travois in the great woods.

His heart pounded, and he felt flushed. He knew what he held in his hand was proof. He knew he'd be asked endless questions in the days to come. He knew the implications of what was jammed into this little bag. Jake stuffed the Ziploc into his shirt pocket and walked back to the house. Jess was still cooking away.

He returned to the bathroom and took a deep breath to calm himself. He looked down at the toilet water and decided the small bag wouldn't clog the pipe if he flushed it.

He took the bag from his pocket and stood in front of the mirror. He stared at his reflection, trying to look himself in the eye.

EPILOGUE

The president made his decision the second Stanton Buckley told him there was no physical evidence. "Then it's a no-brainer, Stan," he said. "We can't go anywhere with this except to minimize it and let the experts sort it out. Let's not get our balls hung out if we're dealing with backwoods tales and no hard evidence. Get our guys out of there and get that prosecuting attorney back on the horn. We need to see what we can do for him. What do you think about a news release? We can say we've heard the rumors and refer to mass hysteria, the Loch Ness Monster, the Abominable Snowman, and—what's that one running around down in Central and South America?—oh yeah, the chupacabra. We could refer to that one. It's some kind of flying devil that sucks the blood out of livestock."

Stanton's press release would also refer to the Australian yowie, European woodwose from medieval times, the Chinese yerin, and Sumatra's orang pendek, in addition to the gruesome chupacabra. In particular, the summary would point out the many true believers of Almas, known as the Russian Bigfoot and described by witnesses as looking like a relic Neanderthal man, said to lurk near the Caucasus Mountains. The White House statement would conclude, "The discovery of a new species of upright bipedal hominid is always a possibility but from a scientific point of view will require irrefutable physical evidence."

———◆———

DID SOMETHING HAPPEN? was the cover headline of *U.S. News & World Report's* special edition the following week. Dave had his cover. It ran above the famous but controversial picture from 1970s videotape of a supposed Sasquatch female striding through a dry creek bed in Northern California. That videotape is sometimes considered a hoax. Dave's story was a maybe-this-maybe-that piece with senior editors trying to balance the claims emanating from Hee-Haw's Tavern by interviewing academics who referred to a lack of empirical evidence. Inside the cover and with his father's encouragement, Dave wrote a first-person account and held back nothing. It began: .

> I found it on the Internet, the source of far more fabrication than truth. When I got there, I talked to everyone involved (those who were willing to talk, anyway). But I still can't be sure whether or not something happened. The folks in Aurora, Washington, believe their own accounts,

that much is clear. All I can do is report them to you.

There are about a dozen men and a couple of women who tell a remarkably similar story about their town being invaded by creatures that aren't supposed to exist. Was a Bigfoot shot and killed and brought to the town? Did a group of the creatures confront the locals and take away the body?

Their stories are consistent in all but the smallest of details. One man isn't talking, however, and has departed for an extended trip to Europe. His name is Jake Holly, and the rumor in Aurora has him accidentally shooting the Bigfoot. I managed to get Holly on his cell phone in Hamburg, Germany, for the briefest of conversations. He said he'd decided not to discuss the rumor and that he was a private person who wanted to remain private. He said he's not planning to be interviewed about anything related to the Sasquatch, as the creature is known in the Pacific Northwest. He's traveling with his fiancée.

Aurora's local prosecuting attorney, Tal O'Reilly, and the county sheriff, Eldo Throckmorton, are even less forthcoming. In a joint interview, which they insisted on, their basic position was that they couldn't, and wouldn't, confirm or deny anything.

O'Reilly said, "We're well aware of the stories floating around, but since we weren't personally there, we don't know what to think."

The sheriff added, "We've known most of these folks a long time, and they're not a bunch of nuts. But we were having a pretty rough night with lots of rain on top of blowing ash and smoke from St. Helens. It was hard to see across the street."

Could the clear-eyed reticence of these men indicate that they're the ones blowing smoke instead of Mount St. Helens? To alter Shakespeare only a little, methinks they doth protest too much.

———— ◆ ————

The sensational supermarket tabloids couldn't be satisfied by simply reporting events percolating from Aurora. They needed to raise the stakes. Under the headline ALIENS KIDNAP BIGFOOT, the *Tattler* ran an imaginative piece with faked pictures explaining how a northwestern Sasquatch had inadvertently been beamed up to a huge spacecraft, examined by the aliens, and returned unharmed. Locals saw the UFO and the Bigfoot beamed up, the story claimed, and went on to speculate how Bigfoot may have prevented an invasion when the aliens saw its size and power.

———•◆•———

The president and Stanton Buckley discussed inviting Tal and Ruth O'Reilly to an upcoming White House dinner, which would be dripping with senators and ambassadors. In the end, they decided against it. They would need to include the sheriff and the undertaker and the two in Europe to cover all bases. That could get complicated. How would they introduce them? What if the press cornered them? Eventually, the president called Tal and told him he appreciated his help in keeping the lid on, even though it certainly appeared something unusual had happened.

"Yes, sir, Mr. President. Something highly unusual," Tal responded.

"Well, you can sure bet our folks will be following this," the president promised. "Without any hard evidence, we just can't see any benefit in trying to confirm it now. Plus, you're going to get your share of crazies out there without any help from us. Tell you what, Tal. You seem like a reasonable man, someone we could work with. I'd like to talk to you and the other folks who helped you make the video and so forth. But if we bring you here, there'll be a big hubbub, and the press will get worked up. Stan and I think we can come up with a reason to visit Seattle right away. Do you think you and the others would enjoy a little visit to Air Force One right out on the tarmac? We've got a little spot there we can kind of control, so we can get you in and out without much fuss. We could have lunch on the plane and have you folks talk about what you saw. How does that sound?"

"Yes, sir, of course. Just let us know the details. My daughter and her fiancé are out of the country, though. I don't know when they'll be back."

"Isn't he the one who supposedly shot it?"

"Yes."

"Then we'll surely want to talk to them somehow. Have they got a phone with them?"

"They sure do. I called them last night."

"Think they'd take a call from us on Air Force One and chat a little?"

"I think they would. They're not inclined to talk about it, but I'm sure they'll talk to you if you ask them."

"Then that's what we'll do. Bring the number, and my boys can get us a secure connection."

———— ◆ ————

During the next two years, Aurora was ground zero of cryptozoology. Business boomed. Most nights, Hee-Haw's was full to overflowing. Albert hired a former Golden Gloves boxer to be his doorman and bouncer. His main job was to get the regulars in. The price of beer and burgers went up a bit. An entrepreneur from Portland bought the old pool hall across from the courthouse and auctioned off the tables. He installed a rival tavern with leather chairs and smoked salmon sandwiches, but attendance was light. Two new convenience stores opened, plus an express version of a chain hotel. A guy in a suit was buying up land on the edge of town near the highway. He wouldn't answer when asked if he was with Walmart.

Experts came from across the United States, Asia, and Europe. They examined and debated the Sasquatch events, or lack of them, in every way possible. The area's cache of big footprints were studied more closely than ever. Foot-anatomy wizards tested plaster casts for flexion, extension, heel and toe pressure, sole ridges, and interaction with subsoil.

Three famous films were trotted out for review. They all purported to show a Sasquatch but were of poor quality and left plenty of room for doubt. Experts studied the films to rule on the gait, speed, and size of the blurry creatures shown. A Hollywood whiz from a studio specializing in computer animation created a 3-D software program he called Kinematics. He focused on motion studies, biomechanics, and such arcane trivia as leg-hinging characteristics of modern apes.

The strands of unidentified hair and bits of stool discovered down through the decades were analyzed all over again. Modern DNA fingerprinting was tried, but all the efforts were inconclusive. It was pointed out that the old samples were probably contaminated. The best that could be offered from the new generation of research was that the samples weren't human or from any known animal. There was always a qualifier. Nothing conclusive.

Sonographic virtuosos revisited tape recordings made by campers from the 1980s to the present. The tapes contained grunts and screeches that were converted to computer images and compared to known species. A true believer among the sound pros made the most committed assessment when he said, "The recorded noises are not human and do not appear to have been faked. Neither are they from any animal known to live in this part of the world. There is evidence of long-range vocalization with the intent to communicate. I conclude the sounds may have been made by an unknown and relatively advanced species."

On and on and around and around, the debates continued. They discussed "bell-shaped curves" and "primate evolution" and "hominid development into *Homo sapiens*" and "mass hysteria" and "lack of incontrovertible evidence" and "history of successful and widespread hoaxes" and "Loch Ness" and "the now-accepted giant squid." For every person who believed the creatures were real, you could find a person who thought it was all bullhockey.

———◆———

Back in Tokyo and New Delhi, Kenzo and Ashok each published a series of articles about their adventures chasing Bigfoot in America. Both had become true believers. Their newspapers didn't muzzle them or expect balance. The editors were open to sensational and provocative treatment of the subject. As a result, their stories were exciting and widely read, albeit only partly true. Unlike Dave Hulett, the enterprising foreigners tracked down Billy Lasswell and related the events in Aurora from his fly-on-the-wall perspective. Billy's point of view was especially dramatic when telling about hiding in a tree and being snatched up and then dropped by a sympathetic Sasquatch.

An enterprising New York publishing house signed Kenzo and Ashok to a cooperative book deal that would at first be available only on the Internet. From their offices far from each other, the reporters followed an outline e-mailed by their editor. They submitted their copy chapter by chapter via the publisher's website. The editor then meticulously merged and rewrote the story. He was careful to retain the accented flavor of their English and their unvarnished enthusiasm for Bigfoot. The book was published in traditional form seven months after the events in Aurora. *Chasing the Monster* easily made the *New York Times* Best Sellers list. The editors of the *Times's* book section required three meetings to decide whether to list it as a work of fiction or nonfiction. In the end, they put it on the nonfiction list with an editor's note explaining their quandary.

———◆———

Hollywood hustlers chased the scuttlebutt from Aurora and constituted an irresistible force. Money talks, and they spread plenty of it around to loosen the tongues of every participant they could find. The first thing to be completed was a documentary on cable TV called *Bigfoot Down: The Shot Heard 'Round the World.*

Oscar Marsh didn't go public until he had the blessing of Jake and Jess and Tal, and then he cashed in. He became a key figure in the Bigfoot phenomena and could demand thousands of dollars to be interviewed. He also was well paid for assisting the writers and producers of the subsequent major movie, *The Sasquatch Disturbance*. It was a box-office hit, a bona fide movie moneymaker, one of the year's top ten.

———◆———

Jess and Jake returned to Aurora in no hurry whatsoever after leaving in no time flat. After indulging in Jessica's gourmet meal Sunday night and putting a major dent in two bottles of wine, a Washington Chardonnay and a Cabernet, they packed clothes, a cell phone, and a laptop and decamped for the airport. They laughed at their own unscripted departure but didn't waver in their belief that fleeing was the right thing to do. On the road, they made calls arranging details to be handled in their absence. Until they got to the airport and found a flight, they had no idea where they were going.

"I can go anywhere by just closing my eyes," Jess said. "But I love you, Jacob. I go where you go."

The capable foreman for Jake's farm, Julio, was contacted and told to make his own decisions for the time being. Julio knew where the house key was hidden. He'd would bring in the mail and watch for e-mails from Jake about details of the ongoing farm operation. Ruthie would cover for Jessica. She'd call Jess's law secretary on Monday morning to let her know about the unexpected trip. No trial dates were pending in the immediate future, so Jess's e-mail instructions could keep things moving from afar.

Jake and Jess were ready for whatever came next—as long as it was far away. They didn't know whether they were going to Hong Kong or Buenos Aires, but they were prepared to be spontaneous. It turned out to be Prague, by way of London. Two business-class travelers had canceled. Jake and

Jess splurged. On the plane, they sipped champagne, napped, and watched a movie with too many chase scenes.

They loved the old-world stateliness of Prague and traveled farther by first-class trains to Berlin, Hamburg, Paris, Zurich, Venice, Florence, and Rome. They found they enjoyed the going as much as the getting there. Jake said half the fun of travel is feeling your body hurtle through space.

They took a call from the president of the United States after the first few days of travel. They told him the complete truth about their experience with the Sasquatch. He was gracious and interested, interrupting several times to ask questions. He told Jake about his own hunting rifle once owned by his grandfather. They told the president they didn't intend to talk about it when they got home. He thought they were smart to handle it that way. He could think of no advantage to talking about it when there was no proof of anything. He gave them a phone number to call if they needed anything further from him.

When Jake proposed marriage, he told Jess her skin made him happy and reminded him of Chinese lanterns because it seemed to glow from the inside. "When I first see you each day, the blood in my veins stops moving," he said.

They were married in a small chapel near the Trevi Fountain in Rome with only clergy as witnesses. Jake wrote a romantic song lyric and sang it to Jessica in his pleasant voice after they were married and alone in the hotel. He sang it to the tune of a 1939 hit by the Ink Spots, "If I Didn't Care." Three days later, they sat in an outdoor café and decided it was time to go home. The calendar had marched into late

June. Reports from Aurora indicated things had calmed down, if only a little.

Back in Aurora, the newlyweds broke the news to Tal and Ruth and were pleased with their enthusiastic reaction.

"A gift will be forthcoming," Ruthie said with a huge grin, "but I'm putting you on notice right now that I expect some good-looking grandchildren. And I don't want to wait ten years."

When Tal's sister Louise found out, she shocked the couple with her generosity. The third night they were back, Louise had an expensive Portland caterer come to Jake's house to prepare an over-the-top, five-course meal with wines just for the two of them. A local violinist played in the candlelit background, and after the meal, a knock at the door signaled the arrival of a liveried carriage driver to whisk them around the farm in a white surrey pulled by a white horse. When they returned to the house, Louise, Tal, and Ruthie were waiting with dessert and coffee and a demand to hear details of their European expedition.

Jake didn't escape the Sasquatch aftermath unscathed. When word got around that the man who shot Bigfoot was back in town, he was besieged with confrontations and telephone calls from journalists and curiosity seekers. He adopted a simple but effective strategy and applied it with consistency. He handed or read to them his printed statement on a small card, then refused to say anything further.

I am aware of recent publicity surrounding
alleged events in the town where I live,
Aurora, Washington. I am also aware that

my name is mentioned in connection with that situation. This is difficult for a private individual who wishes to remain private. We live in a free country, where any person may choose to speak or remain silent. Therefore, I hope you will understand when I choose to offer no comment. I believe anything I might say would only cause confusion. It is not my intention to make anyone's job more difficult. It is only my intention to exercise my right as a private citizen to remain private. Please accept this statement on behalf of myself and my family.

Jessica had her share of confrontations, as well. She simply referred to "my husband's statement" and declined further comment. Tal and Ruthie didn't use written statements but became adept at saying little and walking away. No one could get a word out of Eldo.

On their wedding night in Rome, Jake told Jess about the Ziploc bag that contained Sasquatch bone fragments, tissue, hair, and blood. He hadn't flushed it. He asked what she thought they should do with it. When they unpacked in Aurora, they removed it from Jake's desk drawer and put it in a safe-deposit box at the bank. It would await a future decision.